喚醒你的英文語感！

Get a Feel for English !

喚醒你的英文語感！

Get a Feel for English !

# 王復國
## 理解式文法
### Understanding English Grammar

## 連接詞、介系詞與冠詞 篇

*Conjunctions,*
*Prepositions*
*& Articles*

 貝塔語言出版
Beta Multimedia Publishing

 **IRT** 語言測驗中心
Language Testing Center

作者◎王復國

## 作者序

# 「知其然亦知其所以然」的文法學習新體驗

大多數的人對英文文法都有兩種誤解。其一是以為英文文法就是一大堆教條式的規定；其二是認定文法規則是硬性的限制，毫無道理可言。其實任何語言的文法都只是文法學家依母語人士使用語言的方式所歸納出來的一些規律。文法的原始目的並不在於「限制」語言的使用方式，而在於「提醒」正確的使用方向。換句話說，是先有語言，後有文法，而不是先文法、後語言。至於認為文法沒有道理，則不外有兩個原因：一、因為與自己的母語有差異；二、因為搞不懂那些規則。當知一個語言的運作有一定的規律，必須在一個完整、合理的系統下才可能被使用者「共同」使用，做有效的溝通。因此，在所謂的文法規則背後基本上都會有一定的邏輯。很不幸地，不論是教英文的人或是學英文的人都缺乏這些認識，結果是教的教不好，學的學不會，雙方互相抱怨，你怪我，我怪你，最後就殃及了無辜的文法。

　　不過，雖然英文文法本身很無辜，但是英文文法書的優劣卻關係著學習成果的好壞。坊間的文法書可說是五花八門、琳瑯滿目。有用中文寫的，有用英文寫的；有的厚厚一大本，有的薄薄一小冊。但不論是哪一種都有一個共同的缺點：只列規則，不做解說。只有極少數的文法書試圖針對某些文法規則做出說明，可惜卻常過度簡化，甚至有避重就輕之嫌。當然，坊間也偶爾看得到一些相當具學術水準之文法書，不過其深奧程度並非一般學習者所需，而且其中之專業術語多艱澀難懂，這類書具研究價值卻不實用。

　　「理解式文法系列」叢書恰好能解決以上這些問題。首先，為了不讓讀者看到一大本文法書而倍感壓力，我們特別做了分冊處理。從最重要、最令人頭痛的動詞開始，依次針對名詞與代名詞、形容詞與副詞，以及介系詞、連接詞與冠詞做各別分析探討，並以難度較高的文法與修辭做為結尾。如此，不但可以幫助學習者將各種文法難題各個擊破，提高學習的成就感，而且可以按部就班，全面性地掌握英文文法的精髓。本系列文法書的用字淺顯，條理分明；筆者刻意將文法術語的數量減至最低，並將每一條重要的文法規則都做了最詳細、合理的說明；書中例句的內容也盡量符合一般的日常生活經驗。本系列書最大的目的就是讓讀者「了解」英文文法，希望能幫助讀者達到「知其然亦知其所以然」的境界，最終能夠把「死」的文法自然而然地「活」用於英文中，不再老是擔心犯錯誤。

　　筆者執教二十餘年，屢屢被學生問及何時可將教學內容集結成書。由於多年來一直忙於教學、翻譯、編審等工作，始終沒有太多餘力從事寫作。最近機緣巧合，剛好有了空檔，於是下定決心開始動筆。筆者秉持文法是要被理解而不是用死記的這個原則，盡所能將各種文法規則做詳盡合理的解釋說明。希望本系列能夠對本地及各地以中文為母語的人士在英語學習的過程中有所助益！

# C o n t e n t s

## 第二部分—介系詞

第 **1** 章　　介系詞的種類

第 $2$ 章　　片語介系詞

第 **3** 章　介系詞片語的功能與位置

第 **4** 章　介詞動詞與片語動詞

# 第三部分―冠詞

第 **3** 章　不定冠詞的用法

第 **4** 章　零冠詞與冠詞的省略

# 連接詞

Conjunctions

> **前言**
>
> # 連接詞表達出兩個文法結構間明確的邏輯關係。

## 1. 何謂連接詞？

　　英文的連接詞叫作 conjunction，由字首 con- (together)、字根 -junct- (join) 加上表狀態的名詞字尾 -ion 所組成。由字面上就可以看出連接詞的功能就在於「連接」，而連接的對象可以是字 (words)、片語 (phrases) 或子句 (clauses)。在英文文法中所謂的「連接」其實分為兩個層次：對等連接 (coordinating) 和從屬連接 (subordinating)。對等連接指的是兩個文法地位相當的結構（包括字、片語及子句）間之聯結；從屬連接則指兩個文法位階不同，具主、從之分的結構（主要為子句）間之聯結。

## 2. 連接詞的重要性

　　連接詞為功能詞 (function words) 的一種；雖然它們本身並不具具體的語意內涵 (semantic import)，但是它們卻能夠表達出

兩個文法結構間明確的邏輯關係 (logical relationship)，比如：相同、相反、對照、比較、因果、條件、讓步、目的等。正因有了連接詞，英文的使用得以更簡潔、有力。例如，以下這兩個句子

① John is a teacher.（約翰是老師。）
② Mary is a teacher.（瑪麗是老師。）

就可以藉由連接詞 and 的使用，合而為一：

③ John and Mary are teachers.（約翰和瑪麗是老師。）

也正因有了連接詞，英文的句意更清楚、明瞭。例如，以下這兩個句子

④ He is rich.（他很有錢。）
⑤ He is not happy.（他不快樂。）

可藉由連接詞 though，表達出兩者間看似矛盾的關係：

⑥ Though he is rich, he is not happy.
（雖然他很有錢，但是並不快樂。）

因此，我們可以這麼說，連接詞猶如語言的潤滑劑，它們能夠使

語言的使用較爲流暢，使其更具效率。

　　在本書的第一部分中，我們將依序討論英文兩大類連接詞（即對等連接詞與從屬連接詞）的功能與用法。在必要時，我們會針對各別的連接詞做特別的說明，以幫助讀者確實掌握英文連接詞的正確使用方式。

　　另外，在本書的第二與第三部分中，我們將分別討論英文的其他兩種功能詞：介系詞與冠詞。*同樣地，我們也將以幫助讀者確切了解、充分掌握這兩種功能詞的意義與用法爲前提，來做必要的分析與說明。

---

* 英文共有四種功能詞：代名詞、連接詞、介系詞與冠詞，其中代名詞已在本系列文法書之第二冊「名詞與代名詞篇」做了完整說明。

第 1 章

# 對等連接詞

　　正如我們在前言中提到的，英文的連接詞分爲對等連接詞 (coordinate conjunction) 和從屬連接詞 (subordinate conjunction) 兩大類。對等連接詞顧名思義指的是用來連接兩個文法地位對等的結構（單字、片語、子句）；[註1] 從屬連接詞則用來連接兩個文法位階不對等，有主、從之分的結構（子句）。我們首先討論對等連接詞。

　　英文的對等連接詞分簡單連接詞 (simple conjunction) 和關聯連接詞 (correlative conjunction) 兩種。

## 1 簡單連接詞

　　簡單的對等連接詞指的是單獨一個字的連接詞，包括 and、or、but、yet、so、nor 和 for。原則上這幾個對等連接詞都可用來連接子句，但並非每一個都適合用來連接單字或片語。以下我們就以對等連接詞可聯結的不同文法結構來分析它們的用法。

### A. 用來連接單字的對等連接詞

　　最常用來連接單字的對等連接詞爲 and 和 or。請看例句：

**a1.**　Those girls are <u>young</u> and <u>pretty</u>.
（那些女孩子們既年輕又漂亮。）

**a2.**　Are they <u>students</u> or <u>teachers</u>?
（他們是學生還是老師？）

a1. 句中的 and 用來連接兩個形容詞 young 和 pretty；a2. 句中的 or 用來連接兩個名詞 students 和 teachers。當然，用對等連接詞連接的單字並不限定詞類，只要對等即可。例如：

**a3.** I'll let you know <u>if</u> and <u>when</u> we have reached an agreement.
（如果而且只要我們達成了協議，我就會讓你知道。）

**a4.** You can choose to <u>stay</u> or <u>leave</u>.
（你可以選擇留下來或離開。）

a3. 句中的 and 連接的是從屬連接詞 if 和 when；a4. 句中的 or 連接原形動詞 stay 和 leave。

除了 and 和 or 之外，有時 but 和 yet 也可用來連接單字，例如：

**a5.** She walked <u>quickly</u> but <u>quietly</u>.
（她走得很快但是腳步很輕。）

**a6.** He is a <u>rich</u> yet <u>stingy</u> person.
（他是個有錢卻很小氣的人。）

a5. 句中的 but 連接 quickly 和 quietly 這兩個副詞，而 a6. 句中的 yet 連接 rich 和 stingy 這兩個形容詞。[註2]

## B. 用來連接片語的對等連接詞

與連接單字的對等連接詞相同，較常用來連接片語的也是 and 和 or。請看例句：

**b1.** They <u>came out of the house</u> and <u>danced in the garden</u>.
（他們來到房子外頭，在花園裡跳舞。）

**b2.** You can come <u>before 12:00</u> or <u>after 1:30</u>.
（你可以在十二點以前或一點半以後來。）

b1. 句中的 and 用來連接 came out of the house 和 danced in the garden 這兩個動詞片語；b2. 句中的 or 用來連接 before 12:00 和 after 1:30 這兩個介系詞片語。

另外，but 和 yet 偶爾也會用來連接片語，例如：

**b3.** She'd like <u>to see</u> but <u>not to be seen</u>.
（她想看但是不想被看。）

**b4.** <u>Feeling tired</u> yet <u>not wanting to go to bed</u>, he turned the TV on.
（覺得很累但是卻不想去睡，於是他就把電視打開。）

b3. 句中的 but 連接兩個不定詞片語 to see 和 not to be seen；b4. 句中的 yet 連接兩個分詞形式的構句 Feeling tired 和 not wanting to go to bed。

## C. 用來連接子句的對等連接詞

原則上所有的對等連接詞都可以用來連接子句。請看例句：

**c1.** We're going to Kenting this weekend, and we'll stay there until Monday.

（我們這個週末要去墾丁，而我們會一直待到星期一。）

**c2.** Give me liberty or give me death.

（不自由毋寧死。）

**c3.** I want to go but I can't.

（我想去可是不能去。）

**c4.** He keeps making promises, yet he never keeps them.

（他不斷地做出承諾，但是卻從來不遵守自己的承諾。）

**c5.** I had a terrible headache, so I decided to call in sick.

（我頭很痛，所以決定打電話請病假。）

**c6.** Nobody has asked me to stay, nor do I intend to do so.[註3]

（沒有人要我留下來，我也沒打算這麼做。）

**c7.** You'd better fix the window, for a typhoon is coming.

（你最好把窗戶修一修，因為颱風快來了。）

以上各句中的對等連接詞皆用來連接前後的兩個子句。注意，原則上用對等連接詞連接子句時，應在對等連接詞前加逗號；但是，如 c2. 和 c3. 句所示，若所連接的子句較短時，可將逗號省略，讓句子顯得簡潔有力。

　　另外，注意 c7. 句之對等連接詞 for 的使用方式與時機。首先，須知 for 雖用來表「原因」，但它是對等連接詞，不可與也用來表達原因的從屬連接詞 because 混淆。由於 for 為對等連接詞，因此，如 c7. 句所示，一般必須置於句中；而由 because 所引導的子句則可置於句首或句尾：

**c8.**　He did not come <u>because he was sick</u>. / <u>Because he was sick</u>, he did not come.
（因為他病了，所以沒有來。）

其次，because 一般用來表示產生某結果的必然原因，而 for 則常用來表達推測的原因。試比較：

**c9.**　He did not come to work yesterday <u>because</u> he was sick.
（因為他病了，所以昨天沒有來上班。）

**c10.**　He must have been sick yesterday, <u>for</u> he did not come to work.
（他昨天一定是病了，因為他沒有來上班。）

　　另外，在 for 與 because 都適用的情況下，一般認為 for 較 because 來得正式。試比較：

**c11.**　The boss told Jim to go home, <u>for</u> he looked exhausted.
（老闆叫吉姆回家去，因為他看起來非常疲憊。）

**c12.** The boss told Jim to go home <u>because</u> he looked exhausted.

（因為吉姆看起來非常疲憊，所以老闆叫他回家。）

事實上，除了以上介紹的 and、or、but、yet、so、nor、for 這七個對等連接詞外，許多母語人士在日常口語中也常會把介系詞 plus 當作對等連接詞來用，例如：

**c13.** This notebook has a bigger screen, plus it is much lighter.

（這台筆記型電腦螢幕比較大，而且重量輕許多。）

最後，要提醒讀者，對等連接詞除了用來連接對等的獨立子句之外，有時也會用來連接對等的從屬子句，例如：

**c14.** <u>Since the job was boring</u> and <u>since he didn't really need the money</u>, David decided to quit.

（因為那個工作很無聊而且他也不是真的需要賺那筆錢，所以大衛決定辭職不幹。）

**c15.** I don't know <u>when he left</u> or <u>where he went</u>.

（我不知道他是什麼時候離開的，也不知道他去了哪裡。）

**c16.** Lynn married a husband <u>who was very smart and handsome</u>, but <u>who just stayed home and watched TV all day</u>.

（琳恩嫁了一個聰明又英俊的丈夫，但是他成天就待在家裡面看電視。）

c14. 句中的 and 連接兩個表原因的副詞子句；c15. 句中的 or 連接兩個名詞子句；c16. 句中的 but 連接兩個形容詞子句。（注意，由於 c16. 句中的形容詞子句裡也用了對等連接詞 "and"，因此 but 之前最好加上逗號，以避免產生混淆或誤解。）

## ② 關聯連接詞

關聯連接詞指的是由連接詞與其相關字詞所聯合組成的固定字組。與簡單連接詞相同，由關聯連接詞所連接的項目必須平行對等。常用的關聯連接詞為：both ... and、not only ... but also、not ... but、either ... or 及 neither ... nor。以下分別說明各個關聯連接詞的用法及必須注意的事項。

### A. both ... and

與簡單連接詞 and 的使用情況相同，由 both 和 and 所引導的兩個項目在文法結構上必須對等。請看例句：

**d1.** Both Justin and Elizabeth like music.
（賈斯丁和伊麗莎白兩個人都喜歡音樂。）

**d2.** I came both to see you and to congratulate you.
（我來的目的一方面是看你，一方面要恭喜你。）

**d3.** They hired him both because he is good and because he is the boss's son.
（他們之所以雇用他是因為他不錯，也因為他是老闆的兒子。）

有兩點需要注意，第一，當 both ... and 引導名詞作爲主詞時，動詞須用複數形，如 d1. 句所示。第二，both ... and 不可用在否定敘述中，例如下面 d4. 句即爲錯誤：

**d4.** <u>Both</u> Justin <u>and</u> Elizabeth are <u>not</u> musicians.（誤）
（賈斯丁和伊麗莎白都不是音樂家。）

正確的說法應該是：

**d5.** <u>Neither</u> Justin <u>nor</u> Elizabeth is a musician.

（有關 neither ... nor 的詳細說明請見稍後 E. neither ... nor 一節。）

## B. not only ... but also

not only ... but also 是各類英文測驗中最常考到的相關連接詞，而測試重點一般都在看考生是否能確實了解由 not only 和 but also 所引導的結構必須完全對等。請看例句：

**e1.** Not only <u>you</u> but also <u>I</u> was surprised to see him there.
（不只是你，我也非常驚訝在那兒看到他。）
**e2.** They not only <u>made the rules</u> but also <u>enforced them</u>.
（他們不僅訂定那些規則，而且還嚴格執行。）

**e3.**　Not only <u>did he invite us to his party</u>, but <u>he</u> also <u>gave us gifts</u>.

（他不但邀請我們去參加他的派對，而且還給我們禮物。）

注意，由 not only 與 but also 所引導的兩個項目雖然在文法上必須對等，但是在語意上卻較著重第二項，因此若用來作爲主詞，動詞必須與第二個名詞一致，如 e1. 句所示。註4 另外，若 not only 和 but also 引導的是子句時，記得句首由 Not only 所引導的子句必須採倒裝形式，而第二個子句則應由簡單連接詞 but 來引導，副詞 also 必須置於靠近動詞的位置，不可置於主詞之前，如 e3. 句所示。註5 事實上，也正因爲 also 不是連接詞，所以可以省略不用；換言之，e1.、e2.、e3. 亦可寫成：

**e1'.**　<u>Not only</u> you <u>but</u> I was surprised to see him there.

**e2'.**　They <u>not only</u> made the rules <u>but</u> enforced them.

**e3'.**　<u>Not only</u> did he invite us to his party, <u>but</u> he gave us gifts.

## C. not ... but

簡單連接詞 but 也常與 not 做聯結，形成對照組：not A but B。同樣地，A 項與 B 項必須對等平行。請看例句：

**f1.**　It's not <u>you</u> but <u>George</u> who is to blame.

（該受責備的不是你，而是喬治。）

**f2.** The key was not <u>on the table</u> but <u>in the drawer</u>.

（鑰匙不是在桌上，而是在抽屜裡。）

**f3.** He quit not <u>because he wanted to</u> but <u>because he had to</u>.

（他之所以辭職並不是因為他想辭職，而是因為他必須辭職。）

注意，由於 not A but B 明白表達「主角」為 B，故若涉及動詞，必須與 B 項一致，如 f1. 句所示。

## D. either ... or

either ... or 表達的是「二擇一」的概念，當然被選擇的兩個項目在文法上必須對等。請看例句：

**g1.** Either <u>you</u> or <u>your friend</u> has to be responsible for this.

（不是你就是你的朋友必須為此負責。）

**g2.** He is either <u>at home</u> or <u>at the office</u>.

（他不是在家就是在辦公室。）

**g3.** Either <u>answer my question directly</u>, or <u>shut up</u>.

（要麼直接回答我的問題，否則就閉嘴。）

須要注意的是：若 either ... or 用來引導名詞作為主詞時，動詞必須與 or 之後的名詞一致，如 g1. 句所示。<sup>註6</sup>

## E. neither ... nor

neither ... nor 表達的是「既不……也不」（即「二者皆非」）的概念；也就是說，neither ... nor 的邏輯與 both ... and 的邏輯正好相反。請看例句：

**h1.** Neither <u>you</u> nor <u>Louis</u> needs to come.

（你或路易士兩個都不用來。）

**h2.** I will neither <u>call her</u> nor <u>write her</u>.

（我不會打電話給她，也不會寫信給她。）

**h3.** I like him neither <u>because he is good-looking</u> nor <u>because he is rich</u>.

（我喜歡他並不是因為他長得帥，也不是因為他有錢。）

與 either ... or 相同，用 neither ... nor 引導主詞時，動詞應與 nor 之後的名詞一致，如 h1. 句所示。

## 註解

**1** 事實上，用對等連接詞連接的項目可以是兩個以上，例如：

There are <u>two chairs</u>, <u>a desk</u>(,) and <u>a bed</u> in the room.
（房間裡有兩張椅子、一張書桌和一張床。）

但是為說明上的方便，在本章的例句中我們原則上僅提供兩個項目。

**2** but 和 yet 都用來表達「對照」或「相反」，但是在語氣上 yet 較 but 強烈。

**3** 注意，nor 之後的子句須採倒裝句型。

**4** 注意，若主詞中的兩個項目是由 as well as、no less than 及 together with 這三個慣用語來做聯結的時候，則應以第一項為重，意即，動詞必須與第一個名詞一致：

❶ He as well as his sons is supposed to come to the hearing.
（他還有他的兒子都應該來參加聽證會。）

❷ I no less than you was wrong.
（我跟你一樣都錯了。）

❸ The pilot together with two passengers was killed in the crash.
（駕駛員以及兩名乘客在飛機墜毀時喪生。）

**5** also 通常置於一般動詞之前（如 e3. 句），be 動詞與助動詞之後：

❶ Not only was he a scientist, but he was also a novelist.
（他不僅是個科學家，還是個小說家。）

❷ Not only will he be there, but he will also give a speech.
（他不但會到場，而且還會發表演說。）

**6** 如註解 1 中提到的，有時對等連接詞可用來連接兩個以上的項目，因此較精確的說法應該是：動詞必須與最後一個名詞一致。例如：

Either you or I or John has to give up.
（不是你就是我，要不就是約翰，必須棄權。）

Conjunction
after Article
from Preposition
through
and
which
about
above
who at
since
below
where over
the
a an
under
that
before

before
where
under
who
through
over
from
since at
below
and
Preposition
an
below
Article

第 2 章

從屬連接詞

從屬連接詞主要的功能在於引導從屬子句 (subordinate clause) 並將其與主要子句 (main clause) 聯結起來，形成所謂的複雜句 (complex sentence)。註1 而由從屬連接詞所引導的從屬子句，依其在句中的功能，可分為名詞子句 (noun clause)、形容詞子句 (adjective clause) 和副詞子句 (adverb clause) 三種。以下我們就依所引導之子句的不同，分別說明扮演不同角色的三種從屬連接詞。

## 1 引導名詞子句的從屬連接詞

可用來引導名詞子句的從屬連接詞包括：純連接詞 that、疑問代名詞、疑問形容詞、疑問副詞、複合關係代名詞以及表「是否」之意的連接詞 whether。請看以下分析說明。

### A. 純連接詞 that

用來引導名詞子句的從屬連接詞 that 是最純粹的連接詞，因為它本身並不具任何語意，它的功能純粹就在於引導名詞子句。請看例句：

**a1.** That he has resigned is true.
（他已經辭職這件事是真的。）

**a2.** I know that he has resigned.
（我知道他已經辭職了。）

**a3.** The fact is <u>that he has resigned</u>.

（事實是，他已經辭職了。）

**a4.** The report <u>that he has resigned</u> is quite shocking.

（說他已經辭職的報導相當令人震驚。）

**a5.** Did you hear the rumor <u>that he has resigned</u>?

（你有沒有聽到傳聞說他已經辭職了？）

a1. 句中的 that 子句為該句的主詞；a2. 句中的 that 子句是動詞 know 的受詞；a3. 句中的 that 子句是主詞 The fact 的補語；a4. 句中的 that 子句是主詞 The report 的同位語；a5. 句中的 that 子句是受詞 the rumor 的同位語。

　　注意，由於 a1. 句是以 That he has resigned 這整個子句作為主詞，相對於其後的「述語」（"predicate"，即動詞 is 與主詞補語 true）而言，顯得太長，因此可將其移至句尾，而原主詞位置則由假主詞 It 來填補，但意思不變：

**a6.** <u>It</u> is true <u>that he has resigned</u>.

另外，有<u>些</u>及物動詞為所謂的「與格動詞」(dative verb)，有兩個受詞（直接受詞與間接受詞），而 that 子句也可作為這類動詞的直接受詞：

**a7.** They told <u>me</u> <u>that he has resigned</u>.

（他們告訴我他已經辭職了。）

在 a7. 句中 me 為間接受詞，that he has resigned 則為直接受詞。
註2

　　前面提到，純連接詞 that 本身並不具語意，因此在討論它的用法時，常會碰到這個問題：that 可不可以省略。原則上，that 是可以省略不用的，但是前提是：不可因而產生誤解。就 a1. ～ a7. 句而言，會產生誤解的是 a1. 句，因為一旦把句首的 That 省去，聽者（甚至讀者）有可能會以為 He has resigned 是主要子句或是一個句子，因而造成溝通上的障礙：

**a1'.**　He has resigned is true. （誤）

而 a2. ～ a6. 句則不致產生這種困擾：

**a2'.**　I know he has resigned.
**a3'.**　The fact is he has resigned.
**a4'.**　The report he has resigned is quite shocking.
**a5'.**　Did you hear the rumor he has resigned?
**a6'.**　It is true he has resigned.
**a7'.**　They told me he has resigned.

一般而言，that 子句愈簡短，that 被省略的機率就愈高。不過，有時 that 的省略與否也與個人使用英文的習慣有關，例如，有些母語人士並不喜歡把作為同位語之 that 子句的 that 省略；換言之，他們會選擇 a4. 與 a5. 句，而不用 a4'. 或 a5'. 這種句子。

## B. 疑問代名詞

疑問代名詞 who / whom、what、which 可作為從屬連接詞引導間接問句作為句子的主詞、受詞、補語等。請看例句：

**b1.** Who / Whom you like is none of my business.[註3]
（你喜歡誰不關我的事。）

**b2.** I don't know what made him so angry.
（我不知道是什麼事讓他那麼生氣。）

**b3.** The most important question is which is more suitable for us.
（最重要的問題是哪一個比較適合我們。）

b1. 句中由 Who / Whom 引導的間接問句為主詞名詞子句；b2. 句中由 what 引導的間接問句為動詞 know 的受詞名詞子句；b3. 句中由 which 引導的間接問句為主詞 The most important question 之補語名詞子句。[註4]

## C. 疑問形容詞

疑問形容詞 which、what、whose 也可用來引導作名詞子句用的間接問句，例如：

**c1.** Which one you chose does not make too much difference.
（你選了哪一個並沒有多大的差別。）

**c2.** Please tell me <u>what</u> time it is.

（麻煩你告訴我現在幾點。）

**c3.** My problem is <u>whose</u> car I should wash first.

（我的問題是我應該先洗誰的車子。）

c1. 中由 Which 引導的間接問句為句子的主詞；c2. 中由 what 引導的間接問句為動詞 tell 的直接受詞；c3. 中由 whose 引導的間接問句為主詞 My problem 的補語。

## D. 疑問副詞

與疑問代名詞和疑問形容詞相同，當疑問副詞 when、where、why、how 用來引導間接問句時，亦視為從屬連接詞。請看例句：

**d1.** <u>When or where</u> he was born is still unknown to us.

（他是什麼時候或在哪裡出生的我們還是不知道。）

**d2.** You never talk about <u>why</u> you divorced her.

（你從來沒有談過你為什麼和她離婚。）

**d3.** What I'd like to know is <u>how</u> you got there without a car.

（我想知道的是沒有車子你是怎麼到那個地方的。）

d1. 句的主詞為由 When or where 引導的子句；d2. 句中由 why 引導的子句為介系詞 about 的受詞；d3. 句的 how 子句則為主詞 What I'd like to know 的補語。

## E. 複合關係代名詞

由複合關係代名詞 whoever / whomever、whatever 以及 whichever 所引導的子句一般都作名詞子句用,因此複合關係代名詞也應視為從屬連接詞。請看例句:

**e1.** Whoever needs this can come and get it.[註5]

(任何需要這個東西的人都可以來拿。)

**e2.** You may do whatever you want to do.

(你可以做你想做的任何事。)

**e3.** You can attend whichever of the three classes you like best.

(你可以上這三堂課中你最喜歡的任何一堂。)

e1. 句中的 Whoever 子句為主詞;e2. 句中的 whatever 子句為動詞 do 的受詞;e3. 句中的 whichever 子句為 attend 之受詞。

## F. 表「是否」的連接詞 whether

由從屬連接詞 whether 引導的名詞子句也屬間接問句,不過與以疑問詞引導的間接問句不同:以疑問詞引導的間接問句是以原問句的疑問詞直接作為連接詞,但是由 whether 引導的間接問句原本是所謂的 Yes-No 問句,也就是沒有疑問詞的問句,因此在轉變成間接問句時必須加上表達「是否」的連接詞 whether。與一般名詞子句相同,whether 子句也可作為主詞、受詞、補語

等。請看例句：

**f1.** <u>Whether the disease is contagious</u> is an important matter.

（這種疾病會不會傳染是個很重要的問題。）

**f2.** Nobody knows <u>whether the disease is contagious</u>.

（沒有人知道這種疾病會不會傳染。）

**f3.** The question is <u>whether the disease is contagious</u>.

（問題是這種疾病會不會傳染。）

**f4.** The question <u>whether the disease is contagious</u> remains unanswered.

（這種疾病會不會傳染的這個問題依然沒有答案。）

f1. 句中的 Whether 子句是該句的主詞；f2. 句中的 whether 子句是該句動詞 knows 的受詞；f3. 句中的 whether 子句是該句主詞 The question 的補語；f4. 句中的 whether 子句則是該句主詞 The question 的同位語。

注意，雖然 whether 本身就具有「是否」之意，但是有時為了要強調「是」和「否」，也可以在 whether 子句之後或 whether 之後加上 "or not"，例如：

**f1'.** Whether the disease is contagious <u>or not</u> is an important matter.

**f2'.** Nobody knows whether <u>or not</u> the disease is contagious.

**f3'.**  The question is whether the disease is contagious <u>or</u> <u>not</u>.

**f4'.**  The question whether <u>or not</u> the disease is contagious remains unanswered.

另外，有時 whether 可以用 if 來取代，但是僅限於兩種情況。第一，當該子句是動詞的受詞時，例如：

**f5.**  <u>I'm wondering</u> whether / if they will arrive on time this time.
（我在想，不知道他們這一次會不會準時抵達。）

第二，當該子句出現在表「不確定」意涵的形容詞之後時，例如：

**f6.**  We're <u>not sure</u> whether / if he will come today.
（我們不確定他今天會不會來。）

在以下幾種情況下則不可用 if 來代替 whether。首先，為了避免讓讀者或聽者誤以為是條件句，因此當表「是否」的子句為句子的主詞時，不可用 If 引導，例如：

**f7.**  <u>If</u> he gets promotion doesn't concern me.（誤）
（他是不是能獲得升遷與我無關。）

其次，若表「是否」的子句爲名詞之同位語時亦不可使用 if：

**f8.** The argument _if_ she is beautiful seems meaningless to me.（誤）

（對我而言爭論她美不美是沒有意義的。）

再者，若「是否」子句爲介系詞之受詞時同樣不應使用 if：

**f9.** There was a lot of discussion about _if_ we should continue with the project.（誤）

（對於我們是否應該繼續執行這個案子有許多的討論。）

最後，若「是否」子句簡化成不定詞形式時，只能用 whether 而不可用 if 來引導，例如：

**f10.** They can't decide _if_ to get married now or wait until next year.（誤）

（他們不能決定該現在結婚還是要等到明年。）

由以上的說明可知，若要用來表達「是否」，if 的使用其實是相當受限制的。而事實上，縱使在可以使用 if 的情況下，還要注意前面我們提到的 "or not" 的擺放位置。我們在前面說過，or not 可以置於 whether 子句之後或緊跟著 whether。但是，若是使用 if 來引導「是否」子句，則 or not 只能置於該子句之尾，

而不可直接置於 if 之後。試比較以下四句：

**f11.** I don't know <u>whether</u> this is true <u>or not</u>.

（我不知道這是不是真的。）

**f12.** I don't know <u>whether or not</u> this is true.

**f13.** I don't know <u>if</u> this is true <u>or not</u>.

**f14.** I don't know <u>if or not</u> this is true.（誤）

另外，作為慣用語表達「不論……或不……」時，只能用 "whether ... or not"，而不可用 "if ... or not"：

**f15.** You'll have to leave now <u>whether</u> you like it <u>or not</u>.

（不管你喜不喜歡，你現在都得離開。）

**f16.** You'll have to leave now <u>if</u> you like it <u>or not</u>.（誤）

## 2 引導形容詞子句的從屬連接詞

用來引導形容詞子句的從屬連接詞有關係代名詞、關係形容詞以及關係副詞。請看以下分析說明。

## A. 關係代名詞

關係代名詞包括：who、whom、which 和 that；在句子中關

係代名詞作為連接詞，引導形容詞子句來修飾其先行詞。請看例句：

**g1.** There's <u>the guy</u> <u>who</u> stole my wallet.

（偷走我皮夾的那個傢伙在那兒。）

**g2.** He paid <u>the vender</u> <u>from whom</u> he had bought the hot dog.

（他付錢給賣他熱狗的小販。）

**g3.** <u>The chair</u> <u>which</u> you broke has been repaired.

（你弄壞的那張椅子已經修好了。）

**g4.** Taipei 101 is <u>the tallest building</u> <u>that</u> I have ever seen.

（台北 101 是我所看過的最高的建築物。）

g1. 句中由 who 引導的形容詞子句用來修飾其先行詞 the guy；g2. 句中由 (from) whom 引導的形容詞子句修飾先行詞 the vender；g3. 句中由 which 引導的形容詞子句修飾先行詞 The chair；g4. 句中由 that 引導的形容詞子句則修飾先行詞 the tallest building。

原則上若先行詞為「人」時，關係代名詞用 who（如 g1. 句所示）；若先行詞為事物，則關係代名詞用 which（如 g3. 句所示）。但是須注意以下幾點。第一，若表人的關係代名詞 who 之前有介系詞，則應用受格形式的 whom（如 g2. 句所示），[註6] 但若介系詞未移前，則用主格 who 即可，例如：

**g2'.** He paid the vendor <u>who</u> he had bought the hot dog <u>from</u>.

第二，一般而言 that 可以用來代替 who 或 which，[註7] 例如：

**g1'.** There's <u>the guy</u> that stole my wallet.

**g3'.** <u>The chair</u> that you broke has been repaired.

但是若先行詞前出現強調性的字眼（如最高級形容詞）時，則不論 who 或 which 皆必須改為 that，例如 g4. 句或

**g5.** Armstrong was <u>the first</u> human that has ever set foot on the moon.
（阿姆斯壯是第一個踏上月球的人類。）

第三，若先行詞為「人＋事物」時，則關係代名詞應用 that：

**g6.** Do you know the story about <u>a girl</u> and <u>her dog</u> that traveled around the world?
（你知不知道那個關於一個女孩和她的狗環遊世界的故事？）

最後，注意若關係代名詞在該子句中為動詞或介系詞的受詞時，可以省略不用，例如：

**g7.** She is the girl I like.

（她是我喜歡的女孩。）

**g8.** The company I worked for is going bankrupt.

（我以前工作的那家公司快倒閉了。）

g7. 句中省略了關係代名詞 who / whom；g8. 句中省略了關係代名詞 which。

## B. 關係形容詞

關係形容詞 whose 其實是關係代名詞 who 和 which 的所有格，在句子中也視為引導形容詞子句的從屬連接詞。請看例句：

**h1.** An orphan is a child whose parents have died.

（孤兒就是父母雙亡的小孩。）

**h2.** He drives a car whose bumpers are coming off.

（他開著一輛保險桿都快脫落的車子。）

h1. 句中由 whose 引導的形容詞子句用來修飾先行詞 a child；h2. 句中的 whose 子句則修飾先行詞 a car。

## C. 關係副詞

關係副詞包括：when、where、why 和 how，分別用來引導修飾表時間、地方、原因及方法之先行詞的形容詞子句，因此也

視爲從屬連接詞。請看例句：

**i1.** 1912 was <u>the year</u> <u>when the Republic of China was established</u>.

（西元 1912 年是中華民國建立的那一年。）

**i2.** <u>The apartment house</u> <u>where I used to live</u> has been torn down.

（我以前曾住過的那一棟公寓已經拆掉了。）

**i3.** <u>The reason</u> <u>why they did that</u> was stated in the report.

（他們之所以那麼做的原因報告裡有說明。）

**i4.** I was shocked at <u>the way</u> <u>how he treated his employees</u>.

（他對待員工的方式令我非常震驚。）

i1. 句中的 when 子句用來修飾先行詞 the year；i2. 句中的 where 子句用來修飾先行詞 The apartment house；i3. 句中的 why 子句用來修飾 the reason；i4. 句中的 how 子句用來修飾 the way。[註8]

　　注意，由於關係副詞與先行名詞之間常在意思上有重疊 (when = time、where = place、why = reason、how = way)，因此有時會省略不用。以上面四個例句來說，i1. 與 i2. 句中的先行名詞 the year 和 The apartment house 雖然分別表示某個時間與某個地方，但是因爲並未直接使用 time 和 place 這兩個字，所以其後的關係副詞 when 和 where 並不顯得累贅；反之，i3. 與 i4. 句中的先行名詞卻正是 the reason 和 the way，因此關係副詞 why

和 how 就顯得多餘。換言之，i1.、i2. 句相對地較 i3.、i4. 句來得通順、自然。職是之故，如果將 i3.、i4. 句中的關係副詞拿掉，句子就會較為簡潔、流暢：

> **i3'.** The reason <u>they did that</u> was stated in the report.
> **i4'.** I was shocked at the way <u>he treated his employees</u>.

事實上，為了避免重複，也可以將先行名詞省略而保留 why 與 how：

> **i3".** <u>Why they did that</u> was stated in the report.
> **i4".** I was shocked at <u>how he treated his employees</u>.

不過要注意，這麼一來 i3". 句中的 Why 子句與 i4". 句中的 how 子句就變成了「名詞」子句，而非形容詞子句了──Why 子句為該句的主詞，how 子句則為介系詞 at 的受詞。

## 3 引導副詞子句的從屬連接詞

　　相較於名詞子句與形容詞子句這兩種從屬子句，副詞子句這種從屬子句與主要子句之間的關係要來得複雜得多。依照其功能，副詞子句可分為表時間、表地方、表原因或理由、表條件、表讓步、表程度或範圍、表狀態、表目的、表結果，及表比較等

十種。以下我們就依其所引導的不同副詞子句，分別介紹十種不同的從屬連接詞。

## A. 引導時間子句的從屬連接詞

引導表時間之副詞子句的從屬連接詞有：when、whenever、while、as、before、after、until、till、since、once，以及片語形式的 as soon as 和 as / so long as。請看例句：

**j1.** My parents had gone to bed <u>when I got home last night</u>.
（昨晚我回到家的時候，我爸媽都已經上床睡覺了。）

**j2.** She gets nervous <u>whenever she is on stage</u>.
（不論何時只要上台表演，她都很緊張。）

**j3.** I'll mop the floor <u>while you cook</u>.
（你煮飯的時候，我會拖地板。）

**j4.** I saw her <u>as she was going into the department store</u>.
（在她要進百貨公司的時候，我看到了她。）

**j5.** You'd better finish your homework <u>before you go out and play</u>.
（在你出去玩之前，最好先把功課做完。）

**j6.** He left town <u>after he quit the job</u>.
（在辭職不幹之後，他就離開了這個城鎮。）

**j7.** We waited there <u>until they arrived</u>.
（我們在那裡一直等到他們到達。）

**j8.** I'll keep this for you <u>till you come back</u>.

（我會幫你把這個保存到你回來。）

**j9.** She hasn't found a job <u>since she graduated last year</u>.

（自從她去年畢業之後，一直沒找到工作。）

**j10.** You'll like him <u>once you get to know him</u>.

（只要你認識他之後，你就會喜歡他。）

**j11.** The students started to talk <u>as soon as the teacher left</u>.

（老師一離開，學生們就開始講話。）

**j12.** You'll be safe <u>as / so long as you stay here</u>.

（只要你待在這裡，就會很安全。）

一般而言，時間副詞子句多用來修飾主要子句中之動詞，表達該動詞所呈現之動作或狀態發生的時間。與時間副詞相同，事實上時間副詞子句也可以置於句首：

**j1'.** <u>When I got home last night</u>, my parents had gone to bed.

**j2'.** <u>Whenever she is on stage</u>, she gets nervous.

**j3'.** <u>While you cook</u>, I'll mop the floor.

**j4'.** <u>As she was going into the department store</u>, I saw her.

**j5'.** <u>Before you go out and play</u>, you'd better finish your homework.

**j6'.** <u>After he quit his job</u>, he left town.

**j7'.** <u>Until they arrived</u>, we waited there.

**j8'.**   Till you come back, I'll keep this for you.

**j9'.**   Since she graduated last year, she hasn't found a job.

**j10'.**  Once you get to know him, you'll like him.

**j11'.**  As soon as the teacher left, the students started to talk.

**j12'.**  As / So long as you stay here, you'll be safe.

注意，當時間副詞子句先出現時，一般多在其後才上逗號（如 j1'. ~ j12'. 句所示）；反之，若主要子句在前，則通常不加逗號（如 j1. ~ j12. 句所示）。

除了以上介紹的十二個引導時間子句的連接詞之外，我們也必須注意三個與時間子句息息相關的字組，這三個字組皆由具否定意涵的副詞搭配從屬連接詞而成，它們分別是 hardly ... when、no sooner ... than 與 not ... until。請看例句：

**j13.**   I had hardly touched the doorknob when the door opened suddenly.

（我才剛碰到門把，門就突然開了。）

**j14.**   He had no sooner got into the taxi than the driver drove off.

（他才一上計程車，司機就把車開走了。）

**j15.**   She did not know the importance of health until she fell seriously ill.

（一直到生了重病，她才知道健康的重要。）

事實上，與這三個字組相關的問題是許多英文考試裡的常客，其中最常考的是當這幾個字組中的否定詞置於句首時的情況。我們在本系列文法書之第三冊「形容詞與副詞篇」中就曾提到過，當否定副詞移至句首時，相關子句中的主詞與動詞必須倒裝，這三個字組中的 hardly、no 與 not 當然也不例外：

> **j13'.** <u>Hardly</u> <u>had I touched</u> the doorknob when the door opened suddenly.
>
> **j14'.** <u>No sooner</u> <u>had he got</u> into the taxi than the driver drove off.
>
> **j15'.** <u>Not until</u> she fell seriously ill <u>did she know</u> the importance of health.

除了句型上的變化外（注意 j15'. 句中 until 子句亦須前移），我們也要提醒讀者注意這幾個句子的意思。首先，j13'. 和 j14'.（j13. 與 j14. 亦同）兩句表面上的否定只是一種修辭手法，它們表達的其實是 j13". 和 j14". 的意涵：註9

> **j13".** As soon as I touch the doorknob, the door opened suddenly.
>
> **j14".** As soon as he got into the taxi, the driver drove off.

其次，千萬不可把 j15'. 句中的 "Not until" 這兩個字直接譯成「不

是一直到」，而應理解成「一直到」（見 j15. 句之中譯）。想要了解爲何如此，我們必須先確實掌握 until（till 亦同）這個連接詞所代表的邏輯意義。一般把 until 譯成「一直到」其實是不夠精確的，它真正的意思是「一直到……才不」，試比較 j16. 句與 j17. 句：

**j16.** The little boy cried until his mother came.
（那個小男孩一直哭，到他媽媽來的時候**才不**哭。）

**j17.** The little boy did <u>not</u> cry, until his mother came.[註10]
（那個小男孩一直沒有哭，到他媽媽來的時候**才哭**。）

換句話說，由於 until 本身具否定意涵，因此若在 until 之前出現否定詞 not，就會產生「負負得正」的結果。這一點需要特別注意。

### B. 引導地方子句的從屬連接詞

引導表地方之副詞子句的從屬連接詞主要爲 where 和 wherever。請看例句：

**k1.** The road ends <u>where</u> the trail begins.
（道路在小徑開始的地方就到了盡頭。）

**k2.** The little girl takes her doll with her <u>wherever</u> she goes.
（不管到哪裡那個小女孩都帶著她的娃娃。）

與時間子句相同，地方子句通常用來修飾主要子句的動詞，而且也可置於句首：

**k1'.** <u>Where the trail begins</u>, the road ends.

**k2'.** <u>Wherever she goes</u>, the little girl takes her doll with her.

另外，注意 everywhere、somewhere、anywhere、nowhere 等複合副詞加上 that 也可用來引導表地方的副詞子句：

**k3.** His dog goes <u>everywhere that</u> he goes.

（不論他到哪裡他的狗就跟到哪裡。）

**k4.** Let's sit <u>somewhere that</u> we can have our lunch in peace.

（咱們找個可以安安靜靜吃個午餐的地方。）

**k5.** You can sleep <u>anywhere that</u> you like.

（你喜歡睡哪兒就睡哪兒。）

**k6.** He can go <u>nowhere that</u> he wouldn't be recognized.

（他不管到哪裡都會被認出來。）

而事實上，以上各句中的 that 皆可省略：

**k3'.** His dog goes <u>everywhere</u> he goes.

**k4'.** Let's sit <u>somewhere</u> we can have our lunch in peace.

**k5'.** You can sleep <u>anywhere</u> you like.

**k6'.** He can go <u>nowhere</u> he wouldn't be recognized.

注意，一旦把 that 省略，everywhere、somewhere、anywhere 和 nowhere 等字的功能就相當於從屬連接詞。

## C. 引導原因 / 理由子句的從屬連接詞

引導表原因 / 理由之副詞子句的從屬連接詞有：because、 since 和 as，以及片語形式的 now that、seeing that、in that、 inasmuch / insomuch as、for the reason that、on the ground(s) that 等。請看例句：

**I1.** The game was canceled <u>because</u> it was raining.
（比賽因爲下雨而取消。）

**I2.** We will comply <u>since</u> you insist.
（既然你堅持，那我們就照辦。）

**I3.** He went to bed early <u>as</u> he had nothing else to do.
（由於沒什麼其他的事幹，所以他就早早就寢。）

**I4.** You can stop worrying <u>now that</u> he is back.
（既然他回來了，你可以不用再擔心了。）

**I5.** They went inside <u>seeing that</u> it was getting dark.
（由於天色漸暗，所以他們就進屋裡去了。）

**I6.** Her solution is better <u>in that</u> it is simple and direct.
（她的解決方案比較好，因爲又簡單又直接。）

**17.** He had to give up <u>inasmuch / insomuch as no one seconded his motion</u>.

（由於他提的動議沒有人附議，他只好放棄。）

**18.** They turned me down <u>for the reason that I wasn't a member</u>.

（因為我不是會員，所以遭到他們的拒絕。）

**19.** She's filing for divorce <u>on the ground(s) that he's having an affair</u>.

（她正在訴請離婚，理由是他有外遇。）

原則上，表原因／理由的副詞子句皆可移至句首位置：

**11'.** <u>Because it was raining</u>, the game was canceled.

**12'.** <u>Since you insist</u>, we will comply.

**13'.** <u>As he had nothing else to do</u>, he went to bed early.

**14'.** <u>Now that he is back</u>, you can stop worrying.

**15'.** <u>Seeing that it was getting dark</u>, they went inside.

**16'.** <u>In that it is simple and direct</u>, her solution is better.

**17'.** <u>Inasmuch / Insomuch as no one seconded his motion</u>, he had to give up.

**18'.** <u>For the reason that I wasn't a member</u>, they turned me down.

**19'.** <u>On the ground(s) that he's having an affair</u>, she's filing for divorce.

## D. 引導條件子句的從屬連接詞

　　用來引導表條件之副詞子句的從屬連接詞包括：if、unless (if ... not)，以及片語形式的 in case、as / so long as、on condition (that)、in the event (that)、provided / providing (that) 等。請看例句：

**m1.**　Don't buy it <u>if you don't like it</u>.
（如果你不喜歡它，就不要買。）

**m2.**　I won't go <u>unless you come with me</u>. (= I'll go if you come with me.)
（除非你跟我一起去，否則我不會去。）

**m3.**　Please have the file ready <u>in case they ask to see it</u>.
（以防萬一他們要求要看檔案，請把它準備好。）

**m4.**　We have nothing else to ask for <u>as / so long as you do what you should do</u>.
（只要你做該做的事，我們並沒有其他任何要求。）

**m5.**　I'll come <u>on condition (that) you send me a formal invitation</u>.
（如果你們發正式邀請函給我，我就來。）

**m6.**　What should I do <u>in the event (that) I get sick</u>?
（如果我生病了，該怎麼做？）

**m7.**　We should be able to help you get the job done <u>provided / providing (that) you give us all the necessary information</u>.
（如果你們把所有必要的資訊都提供給我們，我們應該能夠協助你們把事情搞定。）

一般而言，條件子句都可以前移：

**m1'.** <u>If you don't like it</u>, don't buy it.

**m2'.** <u>Unless you come with me</u>, I won't go.（= If you come with me, I'll go.）

**m3'.** <u>In case they ask to see it</u>, please have the file ready.

**m4'.** <u>As / So long as you do what you should do</u>, we have nothing else to ask for.

**m5'.** <u>On condition (that) you send me a formal invitation</u>, I'll come.

**m6'.** <u>In the event (that) I get sick</u>, what should I do?

**m7'.** <u>Provided / Providing (that) you give us all the necessary information</u>, we should be able to help you get the job done.

注意，有時表時間的 when(ever) 和 once 也可用來表示條件，例如：

**m8.** <u>When(ever)</u> it turns cold, his asthma acts up.
（只要天氣變冷，他的氣喘就會發作。）

**m9.** <u>Once</u> you have made your decision, you have to stick to it.
（一旦你做出決定，就必須堅守立場。）

m8. 句就相當於：

**m8'.** <u>If</u> it turns cold, his asthma acts up.

而 m9. 句就等同於：

**m9'.** <u>If</u> you have made your decision, you have to stick to it.

## E. 引導讓步子句的從屬連接詞

　　用來引導表讓步之副詞子句的從屬連接詞有：though、although、while、whereas，以及片語形式的 even though、even if、granted / granting (that)、admitted / admitting (that) 等。請看例句：

**n1.** He decided to give it a try <u>though he knew he might fail</u>.

（雖然他知道可能會失敗，但是他還是決定一試。）

**n2.** She married him <u>although she didn't love him</u>.

（雖然她不愛他，但是還是嫁給了他。）

**n3.** I can't agree with you <u>while I understand your position</u>.

（儘管我了解你的立場，但是我還是無法贊同你。）

**n4.** He wants a daughter <u>whereas his wife prefers a son</u>.

（他想生女兒，然而他太太卻比較喜歡兒子。）

**n5.** They had to go out to work <u>even though it was snowing</u>.

（縱使在下雪，他們還是得外出工作。）

**n6.** You need to eat <u>even if you don't feel like eating</u>.

（即使你不想吃東西，你也得吃。）

**n7.** He can't be a great musician <u>granted / granting (that)</u>
<u>he does have some talent</u>.

（就算他的確有些天分，他還是不能成為偉大的音樂家。）

**n8.** We can't accept your apology <u>admitted / admitting (that)</u>
<u>you have a good reason for what you have done</u>.

（就算你的所作所為有合理的原因，我們還是不能接受
你的道歉。）

基本上，表讓步的副詞子句都可以移至句首：

**n1'.** <u>Though he knew he might fail</u>, he decided to give it a
try.

**n2'.** <u>Although she didn't love him</u>, she married him.

**n3'.** <u>While I understand your position</u>, I can't agree with you.

**n4'.** <u>Whereas his wife prefers a son</u>, he wants a daughter.

**n5'.** <u>Even though it was snowing</u>, they had to go out to work.

**n6'.** <u>Even if you don't feel like eating</u>, you need to eat.

**n7'.** <u>Granted / Granting (that) he does have some talent</u>,
he can't be a great musician.

**n8'.** <u>Admitted / Admitting (that) you have a good reason for</u>
<u>what you have done</u>, we can't accept your apology.

在結束本節的討論之前，我們要特別介紹一個非常有趣也是用來表示讓步的從屬連接詞 albeit（念成 [ɔl`bɪɪt]）。Albeit 這個字由 "al(though) be it" 變化而來，現今多用於正式的文章之中，在其後可以跟 that 也可以省略不用，例如：

**n9.** Albeit (that) we lost the battle, our morale remained high.

（雖然我們打輸了那場戰役，但是我們的士氣依然高昂。）

當然，由 albeit (that) 引導的子句也可以置於主要子句之後：

**n9'.** Our morale remained high albeit (that) we lost the battle.

## F. 引導程度／範圍子句的從屬連接詞

用來引導表程度／範圍之副詞子句的從屬連接詞主要是 as 以及包含 as 的片語 as / so far as 和 in so far / insofar as。請看例句：

**o1.** He became more ambitious as his business got more successful.

（隨著他的事業愈成功，他也變得愈有野心。）

**o2.** All parties gained in this deal as / so far as I know.

（據我所知，在這場交易中各方都獲利。）

**o3.** I will try to help <u>in so far / insofar as</u> it is within my power.

（只要是在我的權限範圍之內，我會盡力協助。）

以上各句的程度／範圍子句皆可移前：

**o1'.** <u>As his business got more successful</u>, he became more ambitious.

**o2'.** <u>As / So far as I know</u>, all parties gained in this deal.

**o3'.** <u>In so far / Insofar as it is within my power</u>, I will try to help.

另外，下面兩句話中包含 degree 和 extent 這兩個字的片語也常用來引導表程度或範圍的副詞子句：

**o4.** Her back pain increased <u>to the degree that</u> it became unbearable.

（她的背部疼痛加劇，到了無法忍受的程度。）

**o5.** His health has deteriorated <u>to the extent that</u> he is no longer able to work.

（他的健康狀況已經惡化到讓他無法再工作的程度。）

## G. 引導狀態子句的從屬連接詞

　　用來引導表狀態之副詞子句的從屬連接詞主要爲 as 以及包含 as 本身的片語式連接詞 as if 與 as though。請看例句：

**p1.**　Mr. Wilson always does <u>as his wife tells him</u>.
　　　（威爾遜先生總是照他老婆的指示行事。）

**p2.**　You look <u>as if you need some sleep</u>.
　　　（你看起來好像需要睡個覺。）

**p3.**　He talked to me <u>as though we had known each other for a long time</u>.
　　　（他跟我講起話來好像我們已經認識了很久的樣子。）

在一般情況下，表狀態的副詞子句較少置於句首，但是如果該子句是用來修飾整個主要子句時，則可出現在句首或句尾，甚至句中，例如：

**p4.**　<u>As you may have known</u>, they got divorced last week.
　　　（或許你已經知道，他們上個禮拜離婚了。）

**p5.**　They got divorced last week, <u>as you may have known</u>.

**p6.**　They, <u>as you may have known</u>, got divorced last week.

　　注意，除了上面提到的 as、as if 和 as though 之外，在日常口語中有許多母語人士會把介系詞 like 當作引導狀態子句的從屬連接詞用，例如：

**p7.** Like I said, she is not qualified for the position.

（就像我之前說的，她的資格並不足以擔任這個職務。）

**p8.** It looks like it's going to rain.

（看起來像是快下雨了。）

p7. 句中的 Like I said 就是 As I mentioned before 的意思；p8. 句中的 like it's going to rain 就相當於 as if it's going to rain。

## H. 引導目的子句的從屬連接詞

引導表目的之副詞子句的從屬連接詞包括片語形式的 so that、in order that、for fear that，以及單一字 lest。請看例句：

**q1.** He sold some of his land so that he might pay his debts.

（他賣了一些地以便還債。）

**q2.** She usually sits in the front row in order that she can see and hear better.

（為了能看能聽得比較清楚，她通常都坐第一排。）

**q3.** We didn't tell her the truth for fear that she might be devastated.

（因為怕她太難過，我們並沒有告訴她真相。）

**q4.** He studied hard lest he should be failed again.

（他用功念書以免又被當掉。）

有幾點必須說明。第一，q1. 句的 so that 和 q2. 句的 in order that 引導的是「肯定」目的子句；q3. 句的 for fear that 與 q4. 句的 lest 引導的是「否定」目的子句。第二，目的子句多置於句尾，但若要強調該目的時，可將其移至句首，比如 q2. 可改成：

**q2'.** <u>In order that she can see and hear better</u>, she usually sits in the front row.

而 q3. 句可改成：

**q3'.** <u>For fear that she might be devastated</u>, we didn't tell her the truth.

第三，有時 so that 的 so 和 in order that 的 in order 可省略不用：

**q1'.** He sold some of his land <u>that</u> he could pay his debts.

**q2".** She usually sits in the front row <u>that</u> she can see and hear better.

最後，注意 q4. 句裡 lest 子句中的 should 可以用 might 代替：

**q4'.** He studied hard lest he <u>might</u> be failed again.

也可省略，即，動詞使用原形：

**q4″.** He studied hard lest he <u>be failed</u> again.

## I. 引導結果子句的從屬連接詞

引導表結果之副詞子句的從屬連接詞爲 so ... that 和 such ... that 這兩個相關字組中的 that。需注意的是，so ... that 的 so 本身是副詞，因此其後須接形容詞或副詞；such ... that 的 such 則爲形容詞，故其後必須有名詞。請看例句：

**r1.** Annie is <u>so</u> hardworking <u>that</u> she always gets the highest grade.

（安妮是如此地用功，所以總是拿到最高分。）

**r2.** Annie works <u>so</u> hard <u>that</u> she always gets the highest grade.

（安妮如此用功地讀書，所以總是拿到最高分。）

**r3.** Annie is <u>such</u> a hardworking student <u>that</u> she always gets the highest grade.

（安妮是如此用功的一個學生，所以總是拿到最高分。）

**r4.** Annie is <u>such</u> a student <u>that</u> she always gets the highest grade.

（安妮就是如此的一個學生，所以總是拿到最高分。）

r1. 句中的 so 之後爲形容詞 hardworking；r2. 句中的 so 之後爲副詞 hard；r3. 句中的 such 之後有被形容詞 hardworking 修飾的名詞 student；r4. 句中的 such 之後則直接跟名詞 (a) student。

一般而言，結果子句通常不置於句首，但是必須注意以下這幾種強調的句型：

**r5.** <u>So hardworking is Annie</u> that she always gets the highest grade.

**r6.** <u>So hardworking a student is Annie</u> that she always gets the highest grade.

**r7.** Annie is <u>so hardworking a student</u> that she always gets the highest grade.

在 r5.、r6. 句中主詞與動詞倒裝；在 r7. 句中冠詞 a 與形容詞 hardworking 對調位置。

## J. 引導比較子句的從屬連接詞

引導表比較之副詞子句的從屬連接詞為 as（同等比較）和 than（優、劣等比較）。請看例句：

**s1.** Henry is as tall <u>as his older brother is</u>.
（亨利和他哥哥一樣高。）

**s2.** He runs a lot faster <u>than I do</u>.
（他跑得比我快得多。）

**s3.** I ate less <u>than she did</u>.
（我吃得比她少。）

注意，在口說時 s1.、s2. 與 s3. 常會講成：

**s1'.** Henry is as tall <u>as his older brother</u>.

**s2'.** He runs a lot faster <u>than me</u>.

**s3'.** I ate less <u>than her</u>.

也就是說，把 as 和 than 當作介系詞用。但是這種用法並不適用於動詞的比較，例如：

**s4.** <u>Take</u> as much as you <u>need</u>.

（你需要多少就拿多少。）

**s5.** This bag <u>costs</u> more than I <u>thought</u>.

（這個袋子比我原來想的貴。）

## 註解

1　以對等連接詞聯結的子句則構成複合句 (compound sentence)。

2　有關與格動詞的相關說明請參考本系列文法書第一冊「動詞篇」之第 1 章「及物動詞與不及物動詞」。

3　在現代英文中較少使用 whom。相關說明請見本系列文法書第二冊「名詞與代名詞篇」第二部分中之第 5 章「疑問代名詞」。

4　注意，若疑問代名詞在原直接問句中為主詞時，轉變為間接問句時

詞序 (word order) 不變，如 b2. 句及 b3. 句。

5　與註解 3 所提相同，在現代英文中較少使用 whomever，即使在該子
　　句中作爲受詞亦然，例如：

Whoever you want to marry is fine by me.
（不管你要娶 / 嫁誰我都沒意見。）

6　表事物的關係代名詞 which 則無此變化：

This is the ATM from which I withdrew the money.
（這一台就是我提錢時使用的提款機。）

7　但是，如果 who 或 which 之前出現介系詞則不可：

❶ He paid the vendor from that he had bought the hot dog.（誤）
❷ This is the ATM from that I withdrew the money.（誤）

8　針對由關係副詞所引導的形容詞子句，在本系列文法書之第三冊「形
　　容詞與副詞篇」第一部分之第 7 章「形容詞子句」中有較詳盡的說明。

9　與修辭相關的各種問題我們將會在本系列文法書最後一冊「文法與
　　修辭篇」中做分析討論。

10　注意，在本句的主要子句之後我們特別加上了逗號。我們如此做的
　　原因是爲了避免讓這個句子產生歧義 (ambiguity)。如果不加逗號，
　　這個句子有可能被解讀成：那個小男孩並沒有一直哭到他媽媽來（才
　　不哭）。（歧義屬修辭問題，我們將在下一冊「文法與修辭篇」書中
　　做探討。）

# 介系詞

Prepositions

> ### 前言
>
> 雖然介系詞是功能詞，但其所產生的作用是無法取代的。

## 1. 何謂介系詞？

　　英文的介系詞叫作 preposition，由字首 pre- (before)、字根 -posit- (put) 加上字尾 -ion (condition) 所組成，意思是「放在其他字詞之前的字詞」。的確，英文的介系詞必須置於名詞或代名詞之前，也正因如此，有些文法學家把我們一般所說的介系詞稱之爲「前置詞」。*介系詞主要的功能在於作爲兩個事物之間的一種「媒介」，點出二者之間所呈現的「關係」，而所謂的「關係」則包括各種時、空關係及不同的邏輯關聯性，例如前後、上下、內外、因果、目的、手段、來源、所有等。介系詞與及物動詞相同，其後必須接受詞，而介系詞加上其受詞即構成所謂的介系詞片語 (prepositional phrase)，在句子中經常作爲名詞或動詞的修飾語；也就是說，介系詞片語常具形容詞或副詞的功能。

## 2. 介系詞的重要性

介系詞為功能詞，雖然不能像名詞、動詞等實詞明確指出某人事物或動作，但是人事物之間的各種關係或由人事物所做出的動作與其他人事物所產生的關聯卻常須藉由介系詞來表達。例如，「書在桌子上」這個命題中的兩個項目「書」與「桌子」之間的關係就必須利用介系詞 on 來呈現：

The book is <u>on the desk</u>.

或像「老師正走進教室」這個陳述中，老師所做的動作「走」和「教室」這個地點之間的關聯則必須藉由介系詞 into 來表示：

The teacher is walking <u>into the classroom</u>.

除此之外，就如我們在「何謂介系詞」中所言，由介系詞加上受詞所形成的片語常可作為修飾語用，表達出一般形容詞或副詞所無法表達的一些狀態或情況，例如：

the picture <u>on the wall</u>（牆上那幅畫）

中的 on the wall。又如：

handle <u>with care</u>（小心地處置）

中的 with care。

也正因為介系詞之後須接受詞，所以介系詞另一個重要的作用就是：可以接在不及物動詞之後，使不及物動詞具有及物動詞的功能。最常見的兩個例子就是 look at 和 listen to：

① He is looking at us.（他正在看我們。）
② I like to listen to music.（我喜歡聽音樂。）

從以上幾點說明來看，我們可以做出如下的結論：雖然介系詞只是功能詞，但是它們所能產生的作用卻是無法取代的。它們猶如人體的關節，沒有關節的手腳是發揮不了任何正常功能的。

在本書的第二部分中，我們將分五章依次討論介系詞的種類、片語介系詞、介系詞片語的功能與位置、介詞動詞與片語動詞，以及含介系詞的慣用語。

---

* 事實上，並非所有語言的介系詞都為前置詞，比如日文的介系詞就屬所謂的「後置詞」(postposition)：六時に "at six o'clock"。

# 介系詞的種類

　　介系詞可分爲兩大類：一般介系詞 (common preposition) 和片語介系詞 (phrasal preposition)。一般介系詞指的是常見的單一字介系詞；片語介系詞指的是由兩個字或兩個以上的字所組成的介系詞。由於介系詞（一般介系詞與片語介系詞皆然）所表達的意涵相當廣泛，爲了能清楚地說明每一種介系詞的用法，我們將兩大類介系詞分兩個章節來討論。在本章中我們先討論一般介系詞。

　　依所表達之意涵的不同，我們將一般介系詞分成表時間、表地方、表方向、表方法或工具、表目的、表所有、表關係、表狀態、表材質、表來源或起源、表相似或類例、表分離、表讓步、表例外，以及表加減功能等十五種，分別介紹於下。

## 1 表時間的介系詞

　　表時間的介系詞有：at、on、in、within、during、through、for、since、from、between、before、after、until、by、around、about 等。

### A. 介系詞 at 的用法

　　at 通常用來表示短暫的時間，例如：

**a1.** He became the CEO of the company <u>at the age</u> of 25.
（他二十五歲時就當上了公司的執行長。）

**a2.** You will receive the check <u>at the end</u> of this month.

（這個月底你會收到支票。）

at 也可用來表示某個時間點，例如：

**a3.** We don't have any vacancy <u>at the moment</u>.

（目前我們並沒有空缺。）

**a4.** I have lunch meeting to attend <u>at noon</u>.

（正午時我有個午餐會議要參加。）

at 還可用來指出精確的時刻，例如：

**a5.** The game is going to start <u>at 3:00</u>.

（比賽將在三點開始。）

**a6.** I went to bed <u>at 11:30</u> last night.

（昨天晚上我十一點半上床睡覺。）

## B. 介系詞 on 的用法

on 通常用來表示某一天，例如：

**a7.** He was born <u>on July 4</u>.

（他是七月四日生的。）

**a8.** Let's meet <u>on Monday</u> to discuss it.

（咱們禮拜一碰個面討論討論。）

注意，on 也可用來指某一天的上午、下午或晚上：

**a9.** She's leaving <u>on Friday morning</u>.

（她將在星期五早上動身。）

**a10.** What do you usually do <u>on Saturday evenings</u>?

（你星期六晚上通常都做什麼？）

## C. 介系詞 in 的用法

in 通常用來表達較長的時間，如月、季節、年、世紀等。請看例句：

**a11.** Laura will be transferred to the marketing department <u>in May</u>.

（蘿拉五月的時候會被調到行銷部。）

**a12.** It's very hot here <u>in summer</u>.

（這裡夏天的時候非常熱。）

**a13.** Professor Davis retired <u>in 1998</u>.

（戴維斯教授在一九九八年的時候退休。）

**a14.** This temple was built <u>in the 18<sup>th</sup> century</u>.

（這座廟是十八世紀的時候興建的。）

除此之外，in 也可以用來指一天中的早上、下午和晚上：

**a15.** Most people go to work <u>in the morning</u>.

（大部分的人都是在早上去上班。）

**a16.** We normally take a coffee break <u>in the afternoon</u>.

（我們通常會在下午的時候休息一下喝個咖啡。）

**a17.** Sometimes I have to work <u>in the evening</u>.

（有時候我晚上得工作。）

但是，在下列幾個句子中用來表達一天中不同時間的單字前須用 at：

**a18.** They got up <u>at dawn</u>.

（他們在拂曉的時候起床。）

**a19.** I never drink coffee <u>at night</u>.

（我從不在晚間喝咖啡。）

**a20.** The pub closes <u>at midnight</u>.

（這家酒館在午夜十二點打烊。）

另外，注意在 dawn、night、midnight（以及前面 a4. 句中的 noon）之前不用加冠詞，但是在 a15. 句中的 morning、a16. 句中的 afternoon 和 a17. 句中的 evening 前須用 the。

## D. 介系詞 within 的用法

within 用來表達「在某一段時間之內」的概念，例如：

**a21.** I'll be back within an hour.

（我會在一個小時之內回來。）

**a22.** This job must be done within this week.

（這項工作一定要在這個星期之內完成。）

注意，介系詞 in 也具有類似的功用。試比較 a21. 與 a23. 句：

**a23.** I'll be back in an hour.

（我一個小時後會回來。）

但是，正如中譯所示，in 著重在「時間的經過」。

## E. 介系詞 during 的用法

during 表達的是「某動作或狀態在某一段時間內發生或斷斷續續發生」的意涵，例如：

**a24.** Some animals sleep during the day.

（有些動物在白天裡睡覺。）

**a25.** He called me several times during my absence.

（我不在的時候，他打了幾次電話給我。）

注意，有時用 in 與 during 意思相仿，例如：

**a26.** The birth rate declined in / during the last decade.

（過去十年生育率下降。）

要用 in 或 during 端視說話者把生育率下降看成過去十年中發生的一件事，還是在過去十年間呈現的一個過程。

## F. 介系詞 through 的用法

through 用來表達「自始至終」的概念，例如：

**a27.** These students studied very hard <u>through</u> the summer vacation.

（這些學生從暑假開始到暑假結束都非常用功。）

試比較 a27. 與 a28.：

**a28.** These students studied very hard <u>during</u> the summer vacation.

（這些學生在暑假期間非常用功。）

如前所述，during 用來表達「在一段期間內」所發生的動作或狀態，而 through 則強調該動作或狀態的發生在某段期間內「自始至終」皆然。

事實上，為了讓這種「從頭到尾」的意涵更加明確，我們還可以使用複合介系詞 throughout，例如：

**a29.** It rained <u>throughout</u> the night.

（雨下了一整個晚上。）

## G. 介系詞 for 的用法

for 通常用來表示動作或狀態持續的時間，例如：

**a30.** I waited <u>for two hours</u>.

（我等了兩個鐘頭。）

**a31.** We haven't seen him <u>for a long time</u>.

（我們已經好久沒看到他了。）

注意，在口說時 for 可以省略，例如：

**a30'.** I waited <u>two hours</u>.

不過，這時的 two hours 應視為時間副詞，而非 waited 的受詞。

## H. 介系詞 since 的用法

since 用來表達「自……以來」或「自……之後」之意，例如：

**a32.** We've been living here <u>since 2001</u>.

（自 2001 年以來，我們一直都住在這裡。）

**a33.** He had been president of the company <u>since 1985</u>.

（自 1985 年之後，他一直擔任公司的總裁。）

有三點須要注意。第一，由於 since 表達的是「自某時間以來或

之後」的概念，因此相對應的動詞多用現在完成（進行）式（如 a32. 句所示）或是過去完成（進行）式（如 a33. 句所示）。第二，在 since 之後應接一「過去時間」，而非「一段時間」。試比較下列兩個句子。

> **a34.** He hasn't eaten anything since <u>the day before yesterday</u>.
>
> （從前天開始，他一直都沒有吃東西。）
>
> **a35.** He hasn't eaten anything since <u>two days</u>. （誤）
>
> （他已經兩天沒有吃東西了。）

a35. 句應改為：

> **a36.** He hasn't eaten anything <u>for</u> two days.

第三，since 也常當連接詞用，其後接表達「過去」動作或狀態的子句，例如：

> **a37.** I haven't seen him <u>since we met last month</u>.
>
> （自從上個月碰過面之後，我就沒再見到他了。）
>
> **a38.** He had been staying with his grandparents <u>since he was five</u>.
>
> （自從五歲之後，他一直跟著祖父母住。）

## I. 介系詞 from 的用法

from 用來表示時間的起點，常與 to（表迄點）連用，例如：

**a39.** The store is open <u>from 10:00 a.m. to 8:00 p.m.</u>
（這家店的營業時間是上午十點到下午八點。）

from 也常與 now、then、this day、that day 等時間連用，但其後通常須接副詞 on，例如：

**a40.** Things around here will be different <u>from now on</u>.
（這裡的情況從現在開始將會有所不同。）

**a41.** We haven't talked to each other <u>from that day on</u>.
（從那天開始之後，我們就沒有再說過話。）

## J. 介系詞 between 的用法

between 用來表示「介於兩個時間之間」，故須與 and 連用，例如：

**a42.** The library will be closed <u>between Christmas and New Year</u>.
（聖誕節至新年期間圖書館將不開放。）

**a43.** I have classes <u>between 9:00 and 12:00</u>.
（我九點到十二點之間有課。）

注意，between ... and 常可用 from ... to 代換，例如 a43. 就相當
於：

> **a44.** I have classes <u>from</u> 9:00 <u>to</u> 12:00.
>
> （我從九點到十二點有課。）

## K. 介系詞 before 的用法

before 用來表達在某一時間之前，例如：

> **a45.** Please have this done <u>before</u> Wednesday.
>
> （請在星期三之前把這件事辦妥。）

before 也常作連接詞用，引導時間子句，例如：

> **a46.** I had finished my homework <u>before</u> I went out.
>
> （在我出去之前已經先把功課做完了。）

## L. 介系詞 after 的用法

after 用來表達在某一時間之後，例如：

> **a47.** The director will have time <u>after</u> 10:00.
>
> （主任十點之後會有時間。）

與 before 相同，after 也可作連接詞用：

**a48.** I got a call from the boss <u>after you'd left</u>.
（在你離開之後，我就接到老闆打來的電話。）

## M. 介系詞 until 的用法

until 用來表達時間的終止點，例如：

**a49.** Can you wait <u>until noon</u>?
（你可不可以等到中午？）

在口說時常用 till 來取代 until：

**a49'.** Can you wait <u>till</u> noon?

另外，until 常當連接詞用：

**a50.** We stayed in the hotel room <u>until it cleared up</u>.
（我們在旅館的房間裡待著，直到天氣放晴。）

同樣，在口說時可以用 till 來代替 until：

**a50'.** We stayed in the hotel room <u>till</u> it cleared up.

## N. 介系詞 by 的用法

by 用來表達「不遲於」(no later than) 之意,例如:

**a51.** Applications should be submitted <u>by May 31</u>.

（申請書必須在五月三十一日前提交。）

而 a51. 句與 a52. 句在意思上並無太大差異:

**a52.** Applications should be submitted <u>before</u> May 31.

## O. 介系詞 around 的用法

around 用來表達「約略」的時間,例如:

**a53.** We'll arrive <u>around 10:30</u>.

（我們大約會在十點半左右抵達。）

## P. 介系詞 about 的用法

與 around 相同,about 也用來表示大約的時間,例如:

**a54.** It's now <u>about midnight</u>.

（現在大約是午夜。）

另外,about 也常用來表約略的時間長短,例如:

**a55.** It takes <u>about</u> twenty minutes to get there.

（到那裡大約要二十分鐘的時間。）

當然，也可以用 around 來表達相同的意思：

**a55'.** It takes <u>around</u> twenty minutes to get there.

## 2 表地方的介系詞

表地方的介系詞包括：at、in、on、over、above、under、below、beneath、underneath、before、behind、after、beside、by、near、between、among、around、across、opposite、against、beyond、inside、outside、within 等。

### A. 介系詞 **at** 的用法

一般而言，at 大約相當於中文的「在……」，例如：

**b1.** Billy is <u>at the library</u>.

（比利在圖書館。）

**b2.** They are staying <u>at the Hilton</u>.

（他們住在希爾頓大飯店。）

at 也常用來指較明確、特定的位置，例如：

**b3.** Jenny is standing <u>at the door</u>.

（珍妮站在門口。）

**b4.** There's a telephone booth <u>at the intersection</u>.

（十字路口的地方有個電話亭。）

## B. 介系詞 **in** 的用法

in 通常用來表示「在……內」，例如：

**b5.** Stay <u>in the house</u>.

（待在房子裡。）

**b6.** He sat <u>in the car</u> and waited.

（他坐在車子裡等。）

相對於 at，in 通常用來指較大的地方，例如：

**b7.** I'll meet you <u>at</u> the front desk <u>in</u> the lobby.

（我會在大廳的櫃檯處和你碰頭。）

**b8.** She works <u>at</u> Yangming Hospital <u>in</u> Taipei.

（她在台北的陽明醫院工作。）

## C. 介系詞 **on** 的用法

on 一般用來指「在……上面」，例如：

**b9.** Your book is <u>on the desk</u>.

（你的書在書桌上。）

**b10.** He is lying <u>on the floor</u>.

（他躺在地板上。）

注意，在較大型的交通工具上，如公車上、火車上、飛機上、輪船上等，要用 on 來表示：

**b11.** He met her <u>on the train</u> to Tainan.

（他在往台南的火車上遇見她。）

**b12.** We all slept <u>on the plane</u>.

（我們都在飛機上睡了覺。）

另外，也要特別注意在街道名稱前應用 on：

**b13.** She lives <u>on Jinhua Street</u>.

（她住在金華街。）

但若有門牌號碼則用 at 表示：

**b14.** She lives <u>at</u> 125 Jinhua Street.

（她住在金華街一百二十五號。）

## D. 介系詞 **over** 的用法

over 用來指「在……上方」，例如：

**b15.** There's a lamp hanging <u>over the dinner table</u>.
（餐桌上方吊著一盞燈。）

**b16.** His office is directly <u>over</u> mine.
（他的辦公室在我的辦公室正上方。）

## E. 介系詞 **above** 的用法

above 指的是「（高於）……之上」，例如：

**b17.** The airplane is flying <u>above</u> the clouds.
（飛機在雲層之上飛行。）

**b18.** The town is only ten feet <u>above</u> sea level.
（那個城鎮只超過海平面十英呎。）

## F. 介系詞 **under** 的用法

under 指「在……下方」，例如：

**b19.** We hid his present <u>under</u> the table.
（我們把他的禮物藏在桌子下面。）

**b20.** Never stand <u>under</u> a tree when it thunders.
（打雷的時候千萬不要站在樹下。）

## G. 介系詞 **below** 的用法

below 用來指「（低於）……之下」，例如：

**b21.** The sun has sunk <u>below the horizon</u>.

（太陽已經落到了地平線之下。）

**b22.** The temperature will drop <u>below zero</u> tonight.

（今天晚上氣溫會降到零度以下。）

## H. 介系詞 **beneath** 的用法

beneath 用來表達「在……底下」之意，例如：

**b23.** We can feel the heat <u>beneath our feet</u>.

（我們可以感覺到腳下的高溫。）

**b24.** They slept <u>beneath the stars</u> at night.

（晚上他們就在繁星之下入眠。）

## I. 介系詞 **underneath** 的用法

underneath 表達的是「在……下面」，例如：

**b25.** She left her key <u>underneath the mat</u>.

（她把鑰匙放在踏墊下面。）

**b26.** He wore a T-shirt <u>underneath the sweater</u>.

（他在毛衣下面穿了一件運動衫。）

## J. 介系詞 **before** 的用法

before 指「在……前面」，例如：

**b27.** Your name comes <u>before mine</u> on the list.
（在名單上你的名字排在我的前面。）

**b28.** He stood <u>before the window</u> looking out at the street.
（他站在窗戶前面看著外面的街道。）

## K. 介系詞 **behind** 的用法

behind 指「在……後面」，例如：

**b29.** Jerry always sits <u>behind me</u> in class.
（傑瑞上課的時候總是坐在我的後面。）

**b30.** She put the broomstick <u>behind the door</u>.
（她把掃把放在門的後面。）

## L. 介系詞 **after** 的用法

after 指的是「在……之後」，例如：

**b31.** We went into the house <u>after him</u>.
（我們在他之後走進屋內。）

**b32.** The post office is three blocks <u>after the department store</u>.
（郵局在百貨公司之後的三個街區處。）

## M. 介系詞 beside 的用法

beside 指「在……旁邊」，例如：

**b33.** Emma is standing <u>beside her husband</u>.

（愛瑪站在她丈夫旁邊。）

**b34.** He put his bag <u>beside the sofa</u> and sat down.

（他把他的袋子放在沙發旁邊，然後坐下來。）

## N. 介系詞 by 的用法

by 也可以用來表示「在……旁邊」，例如：

**b35.** I was sitting <u>by the telephone</u> when you called.

（你打電話來的時候我就坐在電話旁邊。）

**b36.** His children were all there <u>by his sick bed</u>.

（他的小孩都在他的病床邊。）

## O. 介系詞 near 的用法

near 表示「在……附近」，例如：

**b37.** He lives <u>near the school</u>.

（他住在學校附近。）

**b38.** Don't go <u>near the water</u>.

（不要靠近水邊。）

## P. 介系詞 **between** 的用法

between 用來指「在兩者之間」，例如：

**b39.** There's no secret <u>between</u> us.

（我倆之間沒有祕密。）

between 經常和 and 連用：

**b40.** He travels regularly <u>between</u> Taipei <u>and</u> Shanghai.

（他經常往返於台北和上海兩地。）

## Q. 介系詞 **among** 的用法

among 用來表達「三者或三者以上的之間」，[註1] 例如：

**b41.** They divided the money <u>among</u> the five of them.

（他們五個人平分那筆錢。）

**b42.** You need to choose three <u>among</u> them.

（你必須從他們當中選出三個。）

## R. 介系詞 **around** 的用法

around 指「在……的周圍」，例如：

**b43.** There are many trees <u>around</u> the house.

（那棟房子的周圍有許多樹。）

around 也可指「在……附近」，例如：

**b44.** She lives somewhere <u>around</u> Shilin.
（她住在士林附近。）

## S. 介系詞 across 的用法

across 指「在……的另一邊」，例如：

**b45.** There is a convenience store <u>across</u> the street.
（對街有一家便利商店。）

across 也常用來指「從一邊到另一邊」，例如：

**b46.** There are actually three bridges <u>across</u> this river.
（事實上共有三座橋跨越這條河。）

## T. 介系詞 opposite 的用法

opposite 用來表示「在……的對面」，例如：

**b47.** The library is <u>opposite</u> the museum.
（圖書館在博物館的對面。）

**b48.** He took the seat <u>opposite</u> her.
（他在她對面的那個位子坐了下來。）

## U. 介系詞 **against** 的用法

against 用來表示「倚、靠著」，例如：

**b49.** He was leaning <u>against</u> the wall.
（他靠著牆壁站著。）

**b50.** I saw a bicycle propped <u>against</u> the tree.
（我看到一輛腳踏車靠著那棵樹擺著。）

## V. 介系詞 **beyond** 的用法

beyond 用來指「越過……的另一邊」，例如：

**b51.** Do you know what lies <u>beyond</u> the mountains?
（你知不知道山的那一邊是什麼？）

beyond 還可用來指「在……之外」，例如：

**b52.** His reputation has spread far <u>beyond</u> his own country.
（他的名氣已經傳到了他自己國家以外的許多地方。）

## W. 介系詞 **inside** 的用法

inside 用來指「在（某空間）裡面」，例如：

**b53.** What's <u>inside</u> this envelope?
（這個信封裡裝的是什麼？）

一般而言，inside 比 in 強調「裡面」的意涵。試比較 a53. 與 a54.：

**b54.** What's <u>in</u> this envelope?

（這個信封裡有什麼？）

## X. 介系詞 outside 的用法

outside 為 inside 的相反詞，用來指「在……的外面」，例如：

**b55.** They sat at a table <u>outside</u> the café.

（他們坐咖啡廳外面的桌子。）

**b56.** Let's go somewhere <u>outside</u> the city.

（我們到市區外的什麼地方去吧！）

## Y. 介系詞 within 的用法

within 用來指「在……範圍之內」，例如：

**b57.** This pass can only be used <u>within</u> the facility.

（這張通行證僅限於在廠區內使用。）

**b58.** There were no hotels <u>within</u> twenty miles of the airport.

（在機場周圍二十英哩內沒有旅館。）

## 3 表方向的介系詞

用來表方向的介系詞包括：to、toward、for、up、down、around、about、through、across、over、along、past、by、out、into、onto、upon，及 via 等。

### A. 介系詞 to 的用法

to 用來表達「向、往、到」，例如：

**c1.** He's going <u>to London</u> tomorrow.
（他明天要去倫敦。）

to 常和 from 連用，例如：

**c2.** I drove <u>to</u> the airport <u>from</u> my office.
（我從辦公室開車到機場。）

### B. 介系詞 toward[註2] 的用法

toward 表達「朝、向」之意，例如：

**c3.** They were hurrying <u>toward</u> the village.
（他們匆匆地朝那個村落而去。）

**c4.** She's walking <u>toward us</u>.
（她正朝我們走來。）

## C. 介系詞 for 的用法

for 用來表示「目的地」，例如：

**c5.** He left <u>for Tokyo</u> yesterday.
（他昨天動身前往東京。）

**c6.** I'm heading <u>for the library</u>.
（我正要去圖書館。）

## D. 介系詞 up 的用法

up 用來指「向上」之意，例如：

**c7.** The old man walked <u>up the stairs</u> slowly.
（那個老人慢慢地走上樓梯。）

**c8.** The ship sailed <u>up the river</u>.
（那艘船向河的上游駛去。）

## E. 介系詞 down 的用法

down 為 up 的相反詞，指「向下」，例如：

**c9.** The children ran <u>down the hill</u>.
（孩子們跑下山去。）

**c10.** He fell <u>down the stairs</u>.
（他從樓梯上摔下來。）

## F. 介系詞 around[註3] 的用法

around 用來表達「環繞」之意，例如：

**c11.** The Earth moves <u>around</u> the Sun.
（地球繞著太陽轉。）

around 也可用來表示「四處」，例如：

**c12.** We drove <u>around the city</u> looking for a hotel.
（我們開車在市區內四處找旅館。）

## G. 介系詞 about 的用法

about 可用來指「周圍」，例如：

**c13.** She wore a scarf <u>about her neck</u>.
（她的脖子上圍了一條圍巾。）

about 也可指「到處」，例如：

**c14.** Those kids are running <u>about the yard</u>.
（那些小鬼在院子裡跑來跑去。）

## H. 介系詞 through 的用法

through 用來指「穿過」，例如：

**c15.** The train has just passed <u>through</u> a tunnel.

（火車剛剛穿過一個隧道。）

**c16.** He threw my book out <u>through</u> he window.

（他把我的書從窗戶扔了出去。）

## I. 介系詞 across 的用法

across 指的是「橫越」，例如：

**c17.** They swam <u>across</u> the river.

（他們游泳過河。）

**c18.** He came <u>across</u> the street when he saw me.

（他看到我，於是走過街來。）

## J. 介系詞 over 的用法

over 用來指「越過（高處）」，例如：

**c19.** He hurt his foot when trying to jump <u>over</u> the fence.

（在他試圖跳過籬笆時弄傷了腳。）

**c20.** They climbed <u>over</u> the mountain and reached their destination.

（他們越過那座山，到達了目的地。）

## K. 介系詞 **along** 的用法

along 指「沿著」，例如：

**c21.** Just walk <u>along this road</u> and you will find the place.

（只要沿著這條路走，你就會找到那個地方。）

**c22.** They sailed <u>along the east coast</u>.

（他們沿著東海岸航行。）

## L. 介系詞 **past** 的用法

past 用來指「經過」，例如：

**c23.** He walked <u>past my house</u> without stopping.

（他走過了我家，並沒有停下來。）

**c24.** We drove <u>past several gas stations</u> on our way to the airport.

（在我們開車到機場的路上經過了幾個加油站。）

## M. 介系詞 **by** 的用法

與 past 相同，by 也用來指「經過」，例如：

**c25.** She passed <u>by me</u> without noticing me. [註4]

（她經過我身邊可是沒注意到我。）

**c26.** I go <u>by the florist's</u> every day.

（我每天都經過那家花店。）

## N. 介系詞 out 的用法

out 指「向……外面」，例如：

**c27.** He has just gone <u>out</u> the door.

（他剛剛才走出門外。）

**c28.** She's looking <u>out</u> the window.

（她正往窗外望去。）

## O. 介系詞 into 的用法

into 指「進到……裡面」，例如：

**c29.** It started to rain, so they went <u>into</u> the house.

（因為下起雨來，所以他們就進到屋內。）

**c30.** He got <u>into</u> his car and drove away.

（他上了車然後就開走了。）

## P. 介系詞 onto 的用法

onto 指「到……之上」，例如：

**c31.** He jumped <u>onto</u> the moving train.

（他跳上了已經開動的火車。）

**c32.** Mr. Wilson climbed <u>onto</u> the roof to fix the chimney.

（威爾遜先生爬到屋頂上去修理煙囪。）

## Q. 介系詞 **upon** 的用法

upon 可用來指「到……上」，意思相當於 onto，例如：

**c33.** The lamp fell <u>upon / onto</u> the floor.
（燈掉到了地板上。）

但是，upon 也可指「在……上」，與 on 同義，例如：

**c34.** He fell down <u>upon / on</u> his knees.
（他雙膝著地摔倒了。）

## R. 介系詞 **via** 的用法

via 指「經由」，例如：

**c35.** They flew to Australia <u>via</u> Singapore.
（他們經由新加坡飛往澳洲。）

via 也可指「透過」，例如：

**c36.** You can check your bank account <u>via</u> the Internet.
（你可以透過網際網路查看你的銀行帳戶。）

# 4 表方法或工具的介系詞

常用來表示方法或工具的介系詞為 by 和 with。

## A. 介系詞 by 的用法

by 多用來表「方法、手段」，例如：

**d1.** She earns her living <u>by teaching</u>.

（她以教書維生。）

**d2.** Some people get rich <u>by lying and cheating</u>.

（有些人靠說謊和欺騙致富。）

另外，by 常用來指所使用的交通工具，例如：

**d3.** I go to school <u>by bus</u>.

（我搭公車上學。）

**d4.** You can get there <u>by MRT</u>.

（你可以搭乘捷運到那兒。）

但是，注意下面的用法：

**d5.** He goes to work <u>on foot</u>.

（他走路上班。）

## B. 介系詞 with 的用法

with 常用來指使用的工具，例如：

**d6.** She cut the meat <u>with</u> a sharp knife.

（她用一把鋒利的刀子來切肉。）

**d7.** The old man walks <u>with</u> a stick.

（那個老人走路要拄柺杖。）

## 5 表目的的介系詞

常用來表示「目的」的介系詞是 for。請看例句：

**e1.** She went out <u>for</u> a walk.

（她出去外面散步。）

**e2.** They went to China <u>for</u> sightseeing.

（他們到中國觀光旅遊。）

但是，請注意下面兩句的用法：

**e3.** Mr. Davis is away <u>on business</u>.

（戴維斯先生出差去了。）

**e4.** He dropped the cup <u>on purpose</u>.

（他故意把杯子弄掉。）

# 6 表所有或擁有的介系詞

介系詞 of 常用來表「所有」，with 則用來表「擁有」。

## A. 介系詞 of 的用法

**f1.** He is the father <u>of the two children</u>.

（他就是這兩個小孩的父親。）

**f2.** I ran into an old friend <u>of mine</u> at the post office. [註5]

（我在郵局巧遇了我的一位老朋友。）

## B. 介系詞 with 的用法

**f3.** The man <u>with the silver hair</u> is actually pretty young.

（有著一頭銀白頭髮的那個人其實蠻年輕的。）

**f4.** We're looking for a real estate agent <u>with many years of experience</u>.

（我們在尋找一個擁有多年經驗的房地產經紀人。）

# 7 表關係的介系詞

常用來表示「關係」的介系詞是 to 和 with。

## A. 介系詞 **to** 的用法

**g1.**　Are you related <u>to him</u> in any way?

（你跟他有任何親戚關係嗎？）

**g2.**　This computer is not connected <u>to the main system</u>.

（這台電腦和主要系統並不連線。）

## B. 介系詞 **with** 的用法

**g3.**　They keep very good relations <u>with the police</u>.

（他們跟警方保持非常好的關係。）

**g4.**　This issue is connected <u>with the one we discussed last week</u>.

（這個議題和我們上禮拜討論的議題有關聯。）

## 8　表狀態的介系詞

用來表「狀態」的介系詞有 at、in 和 into。

## A. 介系詞 **at** 的用法

**h1.**　They are <u>at dinner</u> right now.

（他們此刻正在用晚餐。）

**h2.** These two countries have been <u>at war</u> for three years.

（這兩個國家已經打了三年的仗。）

## B. 介系詞 in 的用法

**h3.** Do you realize that you're <u>in great danger</u> here?

（你知不知道你在這裡很危險？）

**h4.** Many of them were <u>in tears</u> when they heard the news.

（當他們聽到那個消息的時候，很多人都哭了。）

## C. 介系詞 into 的用法

**h5.** Don't get yourself <u>into trouble</u>.

（不要讓你自己惹上麻煩。）

**h6.** The water has turned <u>into ice</u>.

（水已經結成了冰。）

# 9 表材質的介系詞

用來表「材質」的介系詞有 of 和 from。

## A. 介系詞 of 的用法

製成產品後材料的本質不變時用 of，例如：

**i1.** This table is made <u>of wood</u>.

（這張桌子是木頭做的。）

**i2.** That teapot is made <u>of iron</u>.

（那只茶壺是鐵製的。）

## B. 介系詞 **from** 的用法

製成產品後材料的本質經過變化則用 from，例如：

**i3.** Our wine is made <u>from local grapes</u>.

（我們的酒是用本地的葡萄所釀造的。）

**i4.** Their new carpet is made <u>from recycled PET bottles</u>.

（他們的新地毯是利用回收的寶特瓶製造的。）

## 10 表來源或起源的介系詞

表「來源或起源」可以用 from 或 of。

## A. 介系詞 **from** 的用法

**j1.** <u>Where</u> are you <u>from</u>?

（你是哪裡人？）

**j2.** The water here comes directly <u>from the reservoir</u>.

（這裡的水直接從水庫引過來。）

## B. 介系詞 of 的用法

**j3.** She was born <u>of a wealthy family</u>.

（她出身於一戶有錢人家。）

**j4.** He was a man <u>of a noble origin</u>.

（他是出身名門的人。）

# 11 表相似或類例的介系詞

可用來表「相似或例子」的介系詞有 like 和 as。

## A. 介系詞 like 的用法

**k1.** He lives <u>like</u> a king.

（他過著帝王般的生活。）

**k2.** We are not allowed to keep pets <u>like cats and dogs</u> in the dorm.

（在宿舍裡我們不准養像貓、狗這類的寵物。）

## B. 介系詞 as 的用法

as 常用在同等比較中，例如：

**k3.** She is as smart <u>as her sister</u>.

（她跟她姐姐一樣聰明。）

as 也常與 such 連用，例如：

**k4.** I like outdoor sports <u>such as jogging, hiking, and bicycling</u>.

（我喜歡諸如慢跑、健行和騎腳踏車等這些戶外運動。）

## 12 表分離的介系詞

表「分離」之意的介系詞有 from 和 with。

## A. 介系詞 from 的用法

**I1.** He was forced to be separated <u>from his family</u>.

（他被迫與家人分離。）

**I2.** Two prisoners escaped <u>from jail</u> last night.

（昨天晚上有兩個犯人從看守所脫逃。）

## B. 介系詞 with 的用法

**I3.** She did not want to part <u>with her children</u>.

（她不願意和她的孩子們分開。）

**I4.** He was reluctant to part <u>with any of his possessions</u>.

（他不願意捨棄任何的財物。）

## 13 表讓步的介系詞

表「讓步」的介系詞包括 despite 和 notwithstanding；前者較口語，後者則較正式。請看例句：

**m1.** The game went on <u>despite / notwithstanding</u> the heavy rain.

（縱使雨下得很大，比賽繼續進行。）

**m2.** <u>Despite / Notwithstanding</u> public opposition, they went ahead with the policy.

（儘管大眾反對，他們依然實施了那項政策。）

## 14 表例外的介系詞

用來表「例外」的介系詞為 but 和 except，意思都是「除……之外」。請看例句：

**n1.** Everyone went <u>but / except</u> Tim.

（除了提姆之外，每一個人都去了。）

**n2.** He wouldn't talk to anyone <u>but</u> / <u>except</u> <u>you</u>.

（除了你之外，他不想跟任何人說話。）

# 15 表加減功能的介系詞

表示「加」的介系詞為 plus，表示「減」的介系詞為 minus。請看例句：

**o1.** Three <u>plus</u> <u>four</u> is / equals seven.

（三加四等於七。）

**o2.** Nine <u>minus</u> <u>five</u> is / equals four.

（九減五等於四。）

## 註解

**1** 事實也有人接受在三者或三者以上之間使用 between，尤其是在下列這種多數之間也有「兩兩個別相互」意涵的句子：

There's fierce competition between John, George and Paul.
（在約翰、喬治和保羅之間有激烈的競爭。）

**2** 英式英文拼寫成 towards。

**3** 英式英文用 round。

**4** 注意，passed 爲動詞 pass 之過去式，但發音與介系詞 past 相同。

**5** 本句中的 "an old friend of mine" 屬「雙重所有格」，相關用法請見本系列文法書第二冊「名詞與代名詞篇」中之「所有代名詞」一章。

Conjunction

before
where
under
who

after Article
through
over

from
through Preposition
from

since at

and below

which and

about

above Preposition

who at an

below

below

where over Article

the a an

under

that 第2章

before 片語介系詞

我們在第一章中提到，所謂片語介系詞 (phrasal preposition) 指的是由兩個或兩個以上的字所形成的介系詞。與一般介系詞的用法相同，在片語介系詞之後也必須接受詞，構成所謂的介系詞片語 (prepositional phrase)。要特別提醒讀者注意的是，不可將片語介系詞與介系詞片語搞混。記得，片語介系詞是「介系詞」，介系詞片語則是「片語」。在本章中我們要介紹的是各種不同的片語介系詞，在下一章中我們則將討論介系詞片語的用法。

依所表達之意涵的不同，我們把片語介系詞分成十三種：表地方的片語介系詞、表方向的片語介系詞、表原因或理由的片語介系詞、表目的的片語介系詞、表條件的片語介系詞、表讓步的片語介系詞、表方法或手段的片語介系詞、表程度或範圍的片語介系詞、表關於的片語介系詞、表附加的片語介系詞、表代替的片語介系詞、表例外的片語介系詞，以及表時間的片語介系詞。請看以下分析說明。

## 1 表地方的片語介系詞

表地方的片語介系詞有 in front of、in back of、ahead of、next to 和 close to。

### A. in front of 的用法

in front of 指「在……的（正）前方」，例如：

**a1.** He walked up and stood <u>in front of</u> the audience.

（他走上前去然後站在觀眾前面。）

**a2.** She sits <u>in front of</u> the TV all day long.

（她整天都坐在電視機前。）

in front of 常可用 before 來替代：

**a1'.** He walked up and stood <u>before</u> the audience.

**a2'.** She sits <u>before</u> the TV all day long.

## B. in back of 的用法

in back of 為美式英語，指「在……的後方」，例如：

**a3.** He was hiding <u>in back of</u> the house.

（他躲在房子後面。）

**a4.** There's a parking lot <u>in back of</u> this building.

（在這棟建築物之後有一個停車場。）

in back of 相當於 behind：

**a3'.** He was hiding <u>behind</u> the house.

**a4'.** There's a parking lot <u>behind</u> this building.

## C. ahead of 的用法

ahead of 指「在……之前」，例如：

**a5.** He is running <u>ahead of</u> us.

（他跑在我們前面。）

**a6.** Our company is <u>ahead of</u> others in the field.

（在業界本公司領先其他的公司。）

## D. next to 的用法

next to 指「緊靠、貼近……」，例如：

**a7.** His room is right <u>next to</u> mine.

（他的房間就在我的隔壁。）

**a8.** Owen is sitting <u>next to</u> Donna.

（歐文坐在唐娜的旁邊。）

next to 可用 beside 代替：

**a7'.** His room is right <u>beside</u> mine.

**a8'.** Owen is sitting <u>beside</u> Donna.

## E. close to 的用法

close to 指「靠近……」，例如：

**a9.** My bed is <u>close to</u> the window.

（我的床靠近窗戶。）

**a10.** Don't get <u>close to</u> me ― I have a cold.

（別靠近我──我感冒了。）

以上兩句中的 close to 可用 near 來代替：

**a9'.** My bed is <u>near</u> the window.

**a10'.** Don't get <u>near</u> me ― I have a cold.

## 2 表方向的片語介系詞

表方向的片語介系詞包括 out of、away from、up to、as far as 和 by way of。

### A. out of 的用法

out of 指「從……裡面出來」，例如：

**b1.** He walked <u>out of</u> the office angrily.

（他很生氣地走出辦公室。）

**b2.** We're moving <u>out of</u> this apartment.

（我們將搬出這棟公寓。）

一般把 out of 視為 into 的相反詞。試比較 b1.、b2. 與 b3.、b4.：

**b3.** He walked <u>into</u> the office angrily.

（他很生氣地走進辦公室。）

**b4.** We're moving <u>into</u> this apartment.

（我們將搬入這棟公寓。）

## B. away from 的用法

away from 表達的是「從……離開」，例如：

**b5.** She walked <u>away from the crowd</u>.

（她走離人群。）

**b6.** The enemy troops were moving <u>away from this town</u>.

（敵軍部隊正撤離這個城鎮。）

away from 可視為 toward 的相反詞。試比較 b5.、b6. 與 b7.、b8.：

**b7.** She walked <u>toward</u> the crowd.

（她朝群眾走去。）

**b8.** The enemy troops were moving <u>toward</u> this town.

（敵軍部隊正朝這個城鎮挺進。）

## C. up to 的用法

up to 指「直到……」，例如：

**b9.** We went only <u>up to</u> the old farm and then turned back.
（我們只到了舊農場就折返了。）

**b10.** I can drive you <u>up to</u> the first intersection.
（我可以開車送你到第一個十字路口。）

## D. as far as 的用法

as far as 指「一直到……」，用法大體與 up to 相同，例如：

**b11.** She walked me <u>as far as</u> the post office.
（她陪我一直走到郵局。）

**b12.** The streetcar only goes <u>as far as</u> the 36<sup>th</sup> street.
（電車只到第三十六街。）

## E. by way of 的用法

by way of 指「取道」，例如：

**b13.** They traveled to Tibet <u>by way of</u> Nepal.
（他們取道尼泊爾到西藏旅行。）

by way of 也可指「經由」，例如：

**b14.** He came to California by way of Panama.

（他經由巴拿馬來到了加州。）

b14. 句等同於：

**b14'.** He came to California via Panama.

## 3 表原因或理由的片語介系詞

表原因或理由的片語介系詞包括 because of、due to、owing to、on account of、thanks to 等。

### A. because of 的用法

because of 表示「因為」，例如：

**c1.** The picnic was canceled because of the rain.
（野餐因為下雨而取消。）

**c2.** Because of his poor health, he had to retire early.
（因為身體不好，所以他必須提前退休。）

### B. due to 的用法

due to 指「由於」，與 because of 的意思及用法皆相仿。[註1]

請看例句：

**c3.** The company went bankrupt <u>due to poor management</u>.

（該公司由於經營不善而倒閉。）

**c4.** <u>Due to the budget cut</u>, we were forced to stop providing the service.

（由於預算被刪減，我們被迫停止提供那項服務。）

## C. owing to 的用法

與 because of 和 due to 相同，片語介系詞 owing to 也用來表原因、理由。請看例句：

**c5.** The baseball game was postponed <u>owing to bad weather</u>.

（棒球賽因為天候不佳而延期。）

**c6.** <u>Owing to rising gasoline prices</u>, more and more people are using public transport.

（由於汽油價格不斷上揚，因而有越來越多的人搭乘大眾運輸工具。）

## D. on account of 的用法

on account of 同樣也用來表達「因為」、「由於」之意。請看例句：

**c7.** She decided not to divorce her husband <u>on account</u>
<u>of</u> the children.

（她因爲小孩的緣故，所以決定不跟她丈夫離婚。）

**c8.** <u>On account of</u> the huge order we received, everyone
had to work overtime.

（由於我們收到龐大的訂單，所以每個人都得加班。）

## E. thanks to 的用法

thanks to 是用來表達原因、理由的一個慣用語。請看例句：

**c9.** <u>Thanks to</u> their help and support, the benefit concert
was a great success.

（由於他們的協助與支持，這場慈善音樂會非常成功。）

**c10.** Now she doesn't even talk to me, <u>thanks to your</u>
<u>stupidity</u>.

（因爲你的愚蠢，她現在連話都不跟我說了。）

thanks to 有時可指「幸虧」，例如：

**c11.** <u>Thanks to</u> him, everyone was safe and sound.

（幸虧有他，每一個人都安然無恙。）

# 4 表目的的片語介系詞

表目的的片語介系詞有 for the purpose of、with a view to、for the sake of、for fear of。

## A. for the purpose of 的用法

for the purpose of 指「目的是為了……」，例如：

**d1.** They came to Taiwan <u>for the purpose of setting up a branch office here</u>.

（他們到台灣來的目的是為了要在這裡設立一間分公司。）

**d2.** <u>For the purpose of their research</u>, they decided to move to that area.

（為了要做研究，他們決定搬到那個地區。）

## B. with a view to 的用法

with a view to 也用來表達目的，意思是「為了（做）……」，例如：

**d3.** He moved to Taipei <u>with a view to getting a better job</u>.

（為了找一份比較好的工作，他搬到了台北。）

**d4.** <u>With a view to helping local children with their English</u>, he opened a small bushiban in that remote town.

（為了要幫助當地的孩童學習英語，他在那個偏遠的小鎮開設了一家小補習班。）

## C. for the sake of 的用法

for the sake of 指「為了⋯⋯（的目的）」，例如：

**d5.** We didn't do this <u>for the sake of</u> money.

（我們並不是為了錢而做這件事。）

注意，for the sake of 也用來表達「為了⋯⋯（的緣故）」，例如：

**d6.** <u>For the sake of</u> her family, she has made a lot of sacrifices.

（為了她的家庭，她做了很多犧牲。）

## D. for fear of 的用法

for fear of 用來表達「否定」的目的，意思是「生怕⋯⋯」，例如：

**d7.** I didn't tell her the truth <u>for fear of</u> upsetting her.

（我沒有告訴她實情，因為怕她難過。）

for fear of 也可指「以免⋯⋯」，例如：

**d8.** He avoids going out <u>for fear of</u> being recognized.

（他避免外出，以免被認出來。）

# 5 表條件的片語介系詞

常用來表示條件的片語介系詞是 in case of 和 in the event of。

## A. in case of 的用法

in case of 指「要是……」，例如：

**e1.** Close the window in case of rain.

（要是下雨，就把窗戶關上。）

**e2.** In case of an emergency, you can call this number.

（要是有緊急狀況，你可以打這個電話。）

## B. in the event of 的用法

in the event of 也用來表示條件，指「如果……」，例如：

**e3.** What should we do in the event of an accident?

（如果發生意外，我們該怎麼做？）

**e4.** In the event of bad weather, the ceremony will be held indoors.

（如果天候不佳，典禮將會在室內舉行。）

# 6 表讓步的片語介系詞

用來表示讓步的片語介系詞為 in spite of 和 regardless of。

## A. in spite of 的用法

in spite of 指「儘管……」，例如：

**f1.** <u>In spite of</u> my objections, they put me on the list.
（儘管我反對，他們還是把我列在名單上。）

**f2.** He has achieved a lot <u>in spite of</u> his disabilities.
（儘管他是殘障，他還是有許多成就。）

注意，in spite of 相當於 despite：

**f1'.** <u>Despite</u> my objections, they still put me on the list.

**f2'.** He has achieved a lot <u>despite</u> his disabilities.

## B. regardless of 的用法

regardless of 指「不顧……」，[註2] 例如：

**f3.** He went ahead with his experiment <u>regardless of all warnings</u>.
（他不顧所有的警告，依然進行他的實驗。）

**f4.** <u>Regardless of</u> our protests, they stuck to their original decision.

（他們不顧我們的抗議，堅持他們原來的決定。）

## 7 表方法或手段的片語介系詞

常用來表方法或手段的片語介系詞是 by means of。請看例句：

**g1.** We usually express our thoughts <u>by means of</u> words.

（我們通常藉由語言文字來表達我們的思想。）

**g2.** She worked her way up to the top <u>by means of</u> hard work.

（她靠努力爬到了最高的位置。）

一般而言，by means of 可以直接用 by 來代替：

**g1'.** We usually express our thoughts <u>by</u> words.

**g2'.** She worked her way up to the top <u>by</u> hard work.

# 8 表程度或範圍的片語介系詞

可用來表程度或範圍的片語介系詞有 according to、in accordance with，以及 as for。

## A. according to 的用法

according to 指「根據……」，例如：

**h1.** <u>According to</u> Freud, our dreams represent our hidden desires.

（根據佛洛伊德的說法，我們所作的夢代表了我們潛在的慾望。）

according to 也可指「按照……」，例如：

**h2.** If everything goes <u>according to</u> the plan, we should be able to finish the job by this Friday.

（如果一切按照計畫進行，這個禮拜五之前我們就應該可以完成這項工作。）

## B. in accordance with 的用法

in accordance with 指「依照……」，例如：

**h3.** <u>In accordance with</u> the law, you have the right to remain silent.

（依照法律，你有權保持緘默。）

**h4.** You are required to act <u>in accordance with</u> the contract.

（你必須依照合約行事。）

## C. as for 的用法

as for 指「至於……」，例如：

**h5.** <u>As for</u> the cost, that's a separate issue.

（至於成本，那是另外一個議題。）

**h6.** <u>As for</u> the rest of you, just be here before nine o'clock.

（至於你們其他的人，只要在九點前到這兒就可以了。）

## ⑨ 表關於的片語介系詞

表關於的片語介系詞有 as to、as regards、in / with regard to、with respect to 等。

## A. as to 的用法

as to 指的是「關於」，例如：

**i1.** We will soon make a decision <u>as to whether to accept</u> <u>your terms</u>.

（關於是否要接受你們的條件，我們很快會做出決定。）

**i2.** There's reasonable doubt <u>as to whether he is guilty</u>.

（關於他是否有罪有可議之處。）

## B. as regards 的用法

as regards 亦指「關於」，但較為正式，多用於商業書信中，例如：

**i3.** <u>As regards your subscription</u>, we are not sure why it was canceled.

（關於您的訂閱，我們並不確定為何被取消。）

**i4.** <u>As regards your recent inquiry</u>, we are happy to inform you that we are opening a new outlet in the downtown area next month.

（關於您最近的詢問，我們很高興地跟您報告，我們即將在下個月在市中心設立一個新的經銷點。）

注意，as regards 可用 regarding 來代替：

**i3'.** <u>Regarding</u> your subscription, we are not sure why it was canceled.

**14'.** Regarding your recent inquiry, we are happy to inform you that we are opening a new outlet in the downtown area next month.

## C. in / with regard to 的用法

in / with regard to 同樣用來表達「關於」、「至於」之意,例如:

**15.** In / With regard to the price, there's no disagreement between us.

（至於價錢,我們雙方的看法並沒有不一致。）

**16.** In / With regard to your application, I'm afraid we're unable to offer you the job at the present moment.

（關於您的申請,恐怕此刻我們沒辦法提供您這項工作。）

## D. with respect to 的用法

另一個可用來表達「關於」、「至於」的片語介系詞是 with respect to。請看例句:

**17.** With respect to your proposal, I'm sorry to say that we cannot agree with it.

（關於你的提案,很抱歉我必須說我們並不認同。）

**18.** They have expressed concern with respect to the new policy.

（有關於新的政策,他們已經表示了關切。）

# 10 表附加的片語介系詞

表附加的片語介系詞包括：in addition to、as well as、together with，以及 along with。

## A. in addition to 的用法

in addition to 用來表「除了……之外還……」，例如：

**j1.** <u>In addition to</u> heavy rain, there were also gusty winds.
（除了大雨之外，還有強陣風。）

**j2.** <u>In addition to</u> giving a general introduction, this new book also provides practical knowledge.
（除了有一般性的概論之外，這本新書還提供了實用的知識。）

## B. as well as 的用法

as well as 也可用來表達「除了……之外還……」。請看例句：

**j3.** She has ability <u>as well as</u> beauty.
（除了美貌之外，她還有能力。）

as well as 也可表達「以及」之意：

**j4.** Chris <u>as well as his two younger brothers</u> was arrested by the police last night. <sup>註 3</sup>

（克里斯以及他的兩個弟弟昨天晚上遭警方逮捕。）

## C. together with 的用法

together with 指「與……一起」，例如：

**j5.** The coach <u>together with his team</u> is coming to the party tonight. <sup>註 4</sup>

（教練和他的球隊今晚將一起來參加派對。）

together with 亦可表達「連同」之意：

**j6.** Mail this letter <u>together with the parcel</u>.

（把這封信連同包裹一起寄出去。）

## D. along with 的用法

along with 的意思與用法大體和 together with 相同。請看例句：

**j7.** There was a letter <u>along with the parcel</u>.

（隨同包裹一起寄來的還有一封信。）

**j8.** The driver <u>along with</u> three passengers was killed in the accident. <sup>註5</sup>

（司機連同三個乘客在那場事故中喪生。）

## 11 表代替的片語介系詞

用來表代替的片語介系詞有 instead of、in place of，以及 in lieu of。

### A. instead of 的用法

instead of 指「代替……」，例如：

**k1.** Cathy will go to the meeting <u>instead of</u> me.
（凱西將代替我去開會。）

instead of 也常用來表達「而不（做）……」，例如：

**k2.** You should be studying <u>instead of</u> watching TV.
（你該是在念書，而不是在看電視。）

### B. in place of 的用法

in place of 也用來指「代替」，例如：

**k3.** In place of our regular class, we're going to watch a film today.

（我們今天將看一段影片來代替正課。）

**k4.** Todd volunteers to go in place of her.

（陶德自願代替她去。）

## C. in lieu of 的用法

in lieu of 同樣也用來指「代替」。請看例句：

**k5.** The company offered us extra holidays in lieu of overtime pay.

（公司提供我們額外的假日來代替加班費。）

**k6.** He gave us a check in lieu of cash.

（他給了我們一張支票代替現金。）

## 12 表例外的片語介系詞

表例外的片語介系詞有 except for、with the exception of、apart from、aside from。

## A. except for 的用法

except for 指「除了……之外」，例如：

**11.** This is a good essay <u>except for</u> a few spelling errors.

（除了幾個字拼錯了之外，這篇文章寫得蠻好的。）

**12.** Everyone came <u>except for</u> Jason and Irene.

（除了傑生和艾琳之外，每一個人都來了。）

注意，except for 有時可用 except 代替，但是僅限於當 except for 指「排除某群體中的一個或數個」時。換句話說，就上面的兩句話而言，只有 12. 符合這個條件；也就是，12. 等於 12'：

**12'.** Everyone came <u>except</u> Jason and Irene.

但是下面的 11'. 為錯誤：

**11'.** This is a good essay <u>except</u> a few spelling errors.（誤）

我們再看一組句子：

**13.** It was a wonderful trip <u>except for</u> one minor traffic accident.

（除了發生了一場小小的交通事故外，這是一趟很棒的旅程。）

**14.** He answered all the questions <u>except (for) the last one</u>.

（除了最後一個問題之外，他回答了所有的問題。）

## B. with the exception of 的用法

with the exception of 也指「除了……之外」，等於上面我們提到的 except。請看例句：

**I5.** Everyone passed the examination <u>with the exception of</u> / **except Frank.**
（除了法蘭克之外，每一個人考試都通過了。）

**I6.** All our bags were found <u>with the exception of</u> / **except Jane's.**
（除了珍的包包之外，我們所有人的包包都找到了。）

## C. apart from 的用法

apart from 亦可指「除了……之外」，相當於前面 except for 的第一種用法。請看例句：

**I7.** <u>Apart from</u> / **Except for a couple of slight defects,** this picture is basically a pretty good piece of work.
（除了有幾處小瑕疵外，這幅畫基本上是一件相當好的作品。）

注意，apart from 有時也用來表達「除了……之外還……」：

**I8.** <u>Apart from</u> **baseball,** he also plays tennis.
（除了棒球之外，他還打網球。）

指「除了……之外還……」時，apart from 相當於 in addition to：

**18'.** <u>In addition to</u> baseball, he also plays tennis.

## D. aside from 的用法

aside from 的意思和用法大體與 apart from 相同。請看例句：

**19.** The night was quiet <u>aside from the occasional barking of dogs</u>.

（除了偶爾有狗叫聲外，那晚相當平靜。）

**110.** <u>Aside from the barking of the dogs</u>, there were other noises.

（除了那些狗的叫聲之外，還有其他的噪音。）

## 13 表時間的片語介系詞

可用來表時間的片語介系詞有 prior to、ahead of 和 up to / until。

## A. prior to 的用法

prior to 指「在……之前」，例如：

**m1.** The agenda should be distributed to the participant <u>prior to</u> the meeting.

（議程在會議開始之前就應該分發給與會者。）

**m2.** The plane caught fire <u>prior to</u> taking off.

（飛機在起飛前著火。）

prior to 為正式用語，在口語時可用 before 來取代：

**m1'.** The agenda should be distributed to the participant <u>before</u> the meeting.

**m2'.** The plane caught fire <u>before</u> taking off.

## B. ahead of 的用法

ahead of 亦指「在……之前」。請看例句：

**m3.** They arrived ten minutes <u>ahead of the scheduled time</u>.

（他比預定的時間早到十分鐘。）

**m4.** Registration must be completed one week <u>ahead of the specified date</u>.

（註冊登記手續必須在規定日期的一個星期前完成。）

ahead of 可用 before 代替：

**m3'.** They arrived ten minutes <u>before</u> the scheduled time.

**m4'.** Registration must be completed one week <u>before</u> the specified date.

## C. up to / until 的用法

up to / until 指「直到……」，例如：

**m5.** Rita was here <u>up to / until</u> five minutes ago.
（麗塔一直到五分鐘之前都在這裡。）

**m6.** <u>Up to / Until</u> this day, I haven't received any call from them.
（直到今日，我還沒有接到他們打來的任何電話。）

## 註解

**1** 有些文法學家認為 due to 只能作形容詞用，而且必須用在 be 動詞之後，例如：

His failure <u>was</u> due to his carelessness.
（他的失敗是因為粗心大意而造成的。）

**2** 注意，有些人會使用 irregardless of，而非 regardless of，但是在正式英文中 irregardless of 被視為錯誤。

**3** 注意，以 A as well as B 作為主詞時，動詞應與 A 一致。

**4** 同樣，以 A together B 為主詞時，動詞與 A 一致。

**5** 以 A along with B 為主詞時，動詞亦應與 A 一致。

Conjunction
Article
Preposition
and
which
who at
since
where over
a an
under
that

第 3 章

# 介系詞片語的功能與位置

　　介系詞最重要的特徵在於它們不可單獨使用，而必須在其後接名詞或代名詞作為其受詞，以介系詞片語的形式在句子中出現。在本章中我們將針對介系詞片語在句中所扮演的功能及其出現的位置做深入的探討。我們先看介系詞片語在句子中的功能。

# 1 介系詞片語的功能

　　介系詞片語在句子中可以作為名詞、形容詞或副詞用。

## A. 作名詞用的介系詞片語

　　介系詞片語可作為其他介系詞的受詞，例如：

**a1.** We won't open until <u>after the Chinese New Year holidays</u>.

（我們一直要到春節假期過後才會開門。）

**a2.** She took the hidden money out from <u>under the rug</u>.

（她把藏起來的錢從地毯下拿出來。）

**a3.** He slept for <u>about twelve hours</u>.

（他睡了大約十二個鐘頭。）

**a4.** There are forty seats in <u>between the two aisles</u>.

（在那兩個走道之間有四十個座位。）

在 a1. 句中 after the Chinese New Year holidays 作介系詞 until 的受詞；在 a2. 句中 under the rug 為介系詞 from 的受詞；在 a3. 句中 about twelve hours 為介系詞 for 的受詞；在 a4. 句中 between the two aisles 則是介系詞 in 的受詞。

另外，在口語中介系詞片語也可作為句子的主詞，例如：

**a5.** <u>After midnight</u> is too late to be out.
（午夜之後出去太晚了。）

**a6.** <u>From 10:00 to 10:30</u> is a good time for us to meet.
（十點到十點半是我們碰頭的好時間。）

## B. 作形容詞用的介系詞片語

介系詞片語常作為名詞的修飾語，例如：

**b1.** The man <u>in the red shirt</u> is my friend Johnny.
（那個穿著紅襯衫的人是我的朋友強尼。）

**b2.** Did you see a girl <u>with a dog</u> walk by?
（你有沒有看到帶著一隻狗的女孩走過去？）

**b3.** This is a picture <u>of my old house</u>.
（這是一張我那棟舊房子的照片。）

**b4.** He told me a story <u>about the Second World War</u>.
（他跟我講了一個有關第二次世界大戰的故事。）

b1. 句中的 in the red shirt 用來修飾該句的主詞 The man；b2. 句中的 with a dog 用來修飾動詞 see 的受詞 a girl；b3. 句中的 of my old house 修飾主詞補語 a picture；b4. 句中的 about the Second World War 則修飾動詞 told 的直接受詞 a story。

## C. 作副詞用的介系詞片語

作副詞用的介系詞片語可以修飾動詞、形容詞和副詞。下列四句爲介系詞片語修飾動詞的例子。

**c1.** I teach <u>at a university</u>.

（我在一所大學教書。）

**c2.** The baseball game continued <u>in spite of the rain</u>.

（儘管在下雨，棒球賽仍繼續進行。）

**c3.** She never works <u>on weekends</u>.

（她週末時從不工作。）

**c4.** He joined the swimming team <u>because of her</u>.

（因爲她的緣故，所以他加入了游泳隊。）

c1. 句中的 at a university 用來修飾動詞 teach；c2. 句中的 in spite of the rain 用來修飾動詞 continued；c3. 句中的 on weekends 修飾動詞 works；c4. 句中的 because of her 則修飾 joined。下列四句爲介系詞片語修飾形容詞的例子。

**c5.** He is famous <u>for his cooking skills</u>.

（他以烹飪技巧出名。）

**c6.** She is jealous <u>of her sister</u>.

（她嫉妒她的姐姐。）

**c7.** You were absent <u>from class</u> yesterday.

（你昨天上課缺席。）

**c8.** I'm not familiar <u>with the new software</u>.

（我並不熟悉新的軟體。）

在 c5. 句中 for his cooking skills 修飾形容詞 famous；在 c6. 句中 of her sister 修飾形容詞 jealous；在 c7. 句中 from class 修飾 absent；在 c8. 句中 with the new software 修飾 familiar。以下四句爲介系詞片語修飾副詞的例子。

**c9.** Soon <u>in the future</u> man will be able to travel in space.

（很快地在未來人類就可以到太空旅行。）

**c10.** I remember I put the cup there <u>on the table</u>.

（我記得我把杯子放在那邊的桌上。）

**c11.** My car was towed away <u>to the garage</u>.

（我的車子被拖到修車廠去。）

**c12.** This computer is not good enough <u>for office use</u>.

（這台電腦拿來作辦公用途不夠好。）

c9. 句中的 in the future 用來修飾副詞 Soon；c10. 句中的 on the

table 用來修飾副詞 there；c11. 句中的 to the garage 修飾副詞 away；c12. 句的 for office use 修飾副詞 enough。

在結束介系詞片語之功能的討論之前，我們要再次強調，介系詞片語與片語介系詞是兩個不同的結構。介系詞片語由介系詞加上受詞而形成，在句子中可作為名詞、形容詞或副詞用。片語介系詞雖然也具片語形式，但是它們只是「介系詞」，與一般介系詞相同，其後必須加上受詞形成介系詞「片語」之後，才能在句子中使用。（本節中的例句 c2. 與 c4. 即使用了由片語介系詞形成的介系詞片語。）

另外，由於有些介系詞與部分從屬連接詞具有相當接近的邏輯意涵，因此在使用上容易產生混淆。這一點也必須特別注意。記得，介系詞之後接的是「受詞」，而連接詞後接的是「子句」。試比較下列 c13.、c14.、c15. 句與其後的 c16.、c17.、c18. 句。

**c13.** <u>During</u> his speech, many people fell asleep.

（在他演講的時候，很多人都睡著了。）

**c14.** The barbecue was postponed <u>because of</u> the rain.

（因為下雨，所以烤肉活動延期。）

**c15.** <u>Despite</u> her failure, she still looked very confident.

（儘管她失敗了，她看起來還是非常有自信。）

注意，以上三句中劃底線的字為介系詞，故其後接受詞。

**c16.** <u>While</u> he was giving his speech, many people fell asleep.

（當他在演講的時候，很多人都睡著了。）

**c17.** The barbecue was postponed <u>because</u> it was raining.

（因為在下雨，所以烤肉活動延期。）

**c18.** <u>Although</u> she failed, she still looked very confident.

（儘管她失敗了，但是她看起來還是很有自信。）

以上三句中劃底線的字為連接詞，故其後接的是子句。

## 2 介系詞片語的位置

基本上作名詞與形容詞用的介系詞片語在句子中的位置較為固定，但作為副詞的介系詞片語則因其修飾對象之不同及修辭上的需要會出現在句子中不同的位置。

### A. 名詞介系詞片語的位置

介系詞片語若作為主詞就出現在句首；若作為介系詞之受詞則須緊跟在該介系詞之後。請看例句：

**d1.** <u>Over the top</u> is over the top.

（太超過就太超過了。）

**d2.** The noise is coming from <u>behind the truck</u>.

（聲音是從卡車後面傳出來的。）

## B. 形容詞介系詞片語的位置

作為形容詞用的介系詞片語應跟在被修飾的名詞之後，例如：

**e1.** I have read all the books <u>on the shelf</u>.

（書架上所有的書我都看過。）

當然，介系詞片語中的名詞也可以用介系詞片語來修飾：

**e2.** I have read all the books on the shelf <u>in my room</u>.

（我房間書架上所有的書我都看過。）

e1. 句和 e2. 句中的 on the shelf 都用來修飾 books，而 e2. 句中的 in my room 則用來修飾 shelf。<sup>註 1</sup>

## C. 副詞介系詞片語的位置

修飾形容詞和副詞的介系詞片語通常跟著被修飾的形容詞或副詞，例如：

**f1.** He is not satisfied <u>with the result</u>.

（他對結果並不滿意。）

**f2.** She always gets up very early <u>in the morning</u>.

（她早上都很早起床。）

f1. 句中的 with the result 修飾其前的形容詞 satisfied；f2. 句中的 in the morning 修飾其前的副詞 early。

相對於用來修飾形容詞和副詞的介系詞片語，用來修飾動詞的介系詞片語的位置變化較多。一般而言，修飾動詞用的介系詞片語仍以出現在句尾最為普遍，例如：

**f3.** I usually get up <u>at six</u>.

（我通常六點起床。）

**f4.** He works <u>at a bank</u>.

（他在一家銀行上班。）

**f5.** She went <u>by car</u>.

（她開車去。）

**f6.** They came <u>on business</u>.

（他們來出差。）

但是有三點須要注意。第一，若介系詞片語涉及「單位大小」時，小單位片語置前，大單位片語置後，例如：

**f7.** I usually get up <u>at six</u> <u>in the morning</u>.

（我通常早上六點起床。）

**f8.** He works <u>at a bank</u> <u>in the city</u>.

（他在城市裡的一家銀行上班。）

第二，原則上表地方的片語應置於表時間的片語之前，[註2] 例如：

**f9.** He works <u>at a bank</u> <u>in the daytime</u>.
（他白天在一家銀行上班。）

第三，若還有其他介系詞片語（如表方法、目的等者），則可置於表地方之後，表時間之片語之前，例如：

**f10.** She went <u>to Tainan</u> <u>by car</u> <u>on Wednesday</u>.
（她星期三開車去台南。）

**f11.** They came <u>to Taiwan</u> <u>on business</u> <u>in 2009</u>.
（他們 2009 年的時候來台灣出差。）

不過，以上幾點只是通則，並非絕對，比如表時間的片語就常出現在句首位置：

**f12.** <u>In 2009</u> they came to Taiwan on business.

甚至在句中：

**f12'.** They came <u>in 2009</u> to Taiwan on business.

除了表時間的片語之外，較常出現在句首位置的是具啟承轉合功能的片語，特別是由片語介系詞（如 due to、in spite of 等）所

引導者。請看例句：

**f13.** <u>Due to the power failure</u>, tonight's performance has been canceled.

（由於停電，今天晚上的表演已經取消了。）

**f14.** <u>In spite of his nervousness</u>, he gave a brilliant speech.

（儘管很緊張，他的演說還是非常地精采。）

當然這類的介系詞片語還是可以出現在句尾：

**f13'.** Tonight's performance has been canceled <u>due to the power failure</u>.

**f14'.** He gave a brilliant speech <u>in spite of his nervousness</u>.

也可以出現在句中：

**f13".** Tonight's performance, <u>due to the power failure</u>, has been canceled.

**f14".** He, <u>in spite of his nervousness</u>, gave a brilliant speech.

## 註解

**1** 注意，有時一個名詞會有一個以上的片語修飾語，例如：

I have read all the <u>books</u> <u>about politics</u> <u>on the shelf</u>.
（書架上所有有關政治的書我都看過。）

但是，在一個句子裡應該盡量避免連續使用過多的片語修飾語，以免造成語意不清、理解困難的情況。下面這個句子就容易造成困擾：

I have read all the books <u>about politics</u> <u>in Taiwan</u> <u>on the shelf</u> <u>in my room</u>.（？）
（我房間書架上所有有關台灣政治的書我都看過。）

**2** 事實上，這與一般副詞的情況相同，即，先出現地方副詞，再出現時間副詞：

He goes <u>there</u> <u>every day</u>.
（他每天都去那裡。）

Conjunction
before
where
after Article
under
who
through
from
Preposition
over
through
from
and
since
at
below
which
and
about
above
who at
Preposition
an
below
below
where over
Article
the
a
an
under
that

4

第 4 章

介詞動詞與片語動詞

在本章中我們要討論的是兩種與介系詞相關的動詞：介詞動詞和片語動詞。因為這兩種動詞有時很難區分，所以常會造成學習者的困擾。的確，在許多相關的學習書中經常把這兩類動詞混為一談。從記憶學習的角度來看，或許區分它們並不是很重要；但是就文法理解而言，應有釐清的必要性。所謂介詞動詞 (prepositional verb) 指的是其後加上特定介系詞而成為及物用法的動詞組合。而所謂片語動詞 (phrasal verb) 則指加上一個介系詞或副詞而形成一個與原來動詞意義不同的動詞結構。我們先看介詞動詞。

## 1 介詞動詞

英文裡有一些不及物動詞其後若要接受詞，則必須先加上特定的介系詞，例如在 belong 之後必須接 to：

**a.** This house <u>belongs to</u> Mrs. Brown.
（這棟房子屬於布朗太太所有。）

其他常見的例子包括：

**b.** I don't <u>agree with</u> you.
（我不同意你的看法。）

**c.** You should <u>concentrate on</u> your studies.

（你應該專注在課業上。）

**d.** This committee <u>consists of</u> five members.

（這個委員會由五個成員所組成。）

**e.** Let's <u>listen to</u> some music.

（我們聽點音樂吧！）

**f.** He is <u>looking at</u> the road sign.

（他正看著那個路標。）

**g.** Many people <u>suffer from</u> high blood pressure.

（許多人都患有高血壓。）

**h.** Please <u>wait for</u> me here.

（請在這裡等我。）

注意，以上各例句中的動詞並未因加上了介系詞而改變了它們原來的意思。就文法的層次而言，我們也可以說這些動詞之後的介系詞片語作副詞用，修飾它們前面的動詞。

## 2 片語動詞

前面提到過，片語動詞由動詞加上介系詞或是副詞[註1]而成，因此也常被稱為雙字動詞 (two-word verb)。[註2] 片語動詞與介詞動詞最大的差異在於片語動詞的意思與原動詞的意思不同；也就是說，它們屬全新的字詞。英文裡有相當多的片語動詞，而絕大

多數的片語動詞皆屬所謂的「慣用語」(idiom)。一般而言，片語動詞多用於日常對話中，常可用來取代較正式的用語，例如用 call up 來指 telephone，用 put off 來指 postpone 等。以下我們將就與文法相關的幾個角度來探討英文的片語動詞。

## A. 及物與不及物片語動詞

有些片語動詞後可接受詞，有些則不接受詞。試比較 i. 句與 j. 句：

**i.** She brought up <u>ten children</u>.

（她養育了十個小孩。）

**j.** He suddenly showed up.

（他突然現身。）

i. 句中的 brought up 為及物片語動詞，而 ten children 為其受詞；j. 句中的 showed up 則為不及物片語動詞，故無受詞。我們再看一組對照句：

**k.** I can't figure out <u>why he did that</u>.

（我搞不懂他為什麼那麼做。）

**l.** Do you know why he dropped out?

（你知不知道他為什麼輟學？）

k. 句中的 figure out 為及物，以 why he did that 為受詞；l. 句中

的 dropped out 為不及物，不須受詞。

常用的及物片語動詞還包括：

turn off「關掉」
call off「取消」
draw up「起草」
give up「放棄」
work up「鼓起」
stand for「代表」
rule out「排除」
run into「巧遇」
tear down「拆除」
put together「組裝」

常用的不及物片語動詞還包括：

back down「退縮」
hold on「稍候」
catch on「流行」
pass out「暈厥」
go out「熄滅」
stay up「熬夜」
let up「減弱」

come about「發生」

stick around「逗留」

fall apart「散掉」

## B. 可分離與不可分離片語動詞

　　有些及物片語動詞的受詞可以置於動詞與介／副詞之間，例如前面我們列出的 turn off、tear down 就屬可分離之片語動詞 (separable phrasal verb)。請看例句：

**m.** He turned <u>the light</u> off.
（他把燈關掉。）

**n.** They torn <u>the house</u> down.
（他們把房子拆掉。）

當然，如果一個片語動詞「可」分離，我們也可以選擇「不」分離；也就是說，上面的 m.、n. 兩句可寫／說成：

**m'.** He turned off <u>the light</u>.

**n'.** They torn down <u>the house</u>.

但是要注意，有少數及物片語動詞的受詞永遠必須置於動詞與介／副詞之間，例如：

**o.** My mother talked <u>my father</u> into buying a car for me.

（我媽媽說服我爸爸買了一輛車給我。）

**p.** The gatekeeper let <u>that reporter</u> through.

（看門的人讓那個記者進去。）

而下面的寫／說法為錯誤：

**o'.** My mother <u>talked into</u> my father buying a car for me.（誤）

**p'.** The gatekeeper <u>let through</u> that reporter.（誤）

不過，有趣的是當這些片語動詞被改為被動式時，它們就「不需」分離了：

**o".** My father <u>was talked into</u> buying me a car by my mother.

**p".** That reporter <u>was let through</u> by the gatekeeper.

這是因為原來片語動詞的受詞已經移置句首變成了主詞。

　　相對於可分離的片語動詞當然就是不可分離片語動詞 (inseparable phrasal verb)，而所謂不可分離片語動詞指的是受詞必須置於介／副詞之後的及物片語動詞，[註3] 例如我們前面列出的 stand for、run into 即屬不可分離之片語動詞。請看例句：

**q.** A national flag stands for a country.

（國旗代表國家。）

**r.** I ran into an old friend the other day.

（前兩天我碰到一個老朋友。）

以下兩句為錯誤：

**q'.** A national flag stands <u>a country</u> for.（誤）

**r'.** I ran <u>an old friend</u> into the other day.（誤）

常見的可分離片語動詞還包括：

carry out「執行」

find out「發現」

turn on「打開」

put on「穿上」

cut off「切斷」

pay off「付清」

use up「耗盡」

clear up「釐清」

hand over「交付」

put away「收好」

常見的不可分離片語動詞還包括：

care for「喜歡」

go for「追求」

call for「需要」

count on「依靠」

pick on「找碴」

see to「辦理」

stick to「堅守」

come across「偶遇」

look after「照料」

look into「調查」

## c. 較長的受詞與代名詞受詞的位置

　　雖然可分離片語動詞的受詞可置於動詞與介／副詞之間或介／副詞之後，但是有兩種情況必須注意。第一，當受詞較長、結構較複雜時，為了防止意思不清或造成理解上的困擾，一般都會把這樣的受詞放在介／副詞之後，例如：

**s.** They <u>turned down</u> the man who made the request that
he be exempt from military service.

（他們拒絕了那個提出免除兵役要求的人。）

這麼做的目的在於讓對方（特別是聽者）明確知道這個句子的主要動詞是個片語動詞 (turned down)，而不致於像下面 s'. 句一樣，讓人可能先誤解以為主要動詞是 turned，或不知是 turned … in、turned … into、turned … off 等，而要一直到句子結尾時才發現原來是 turned … down。

**s'.** They <u>turned</u> the man who made the request that he be exempt from military service <u>down</u>. (？)

我們再看一組對照句：

**t.** She <u>put on</u> the dress that she wore on her first date with her first boyfriend twenty years ago.

（她穿上了那件二十年前她第一次和第一個男朋友約會時穿的洋裝。）

**t'.** She <u>put</u> the dress that she wore on her first date with her first boyfriend twenty years ago <u>on</u>. (？)

很明顯地，t. 句要比 t'. 句來得清楚、容易了解得多。

與片語動詞之受詞有關的第二個須注意的狀況是，若受詞為代名詞則一定得置於動詞與介 / 副詞之間。比如，如果我們把 s. 句中的受詞 the man who made the request that he be exempt from military service 換成代名詞 him 的話，則該句應寫／說成：

**u.** They turned <u>him</u> down.

（他們拒絕了他。）

而不可寫／說成：

**u'.** They turned down <u>him</u>.（誤）

同樣，如果把 t. 句中的 the dress that she wore on her first date with her first boyfriend twenty years ago 換成 it 的話，該句會是：

**v.** She put <u>it</u> on.

而不應是：

**v'.** She put on <u>it</u>.（誤）

這一點請務必留意。

## D. 三字片語動詞

如我們在註解 2 中所提到的，事實上片語動詞並不限於兩個字，有些片語動詞是由三個字所組成。一般而言，三字片語動詞

(three-word phrasal verb) 多是由動詞加副詞再加上介系詞所形成，例如 come up with、run out of、look forward to 等。請看例句：

**w.** After thinking for one whole week, he finally <u>came up with</u> a solution.

（在想了一整個禮拜之後，他終於想出了解決之道。）

**x.** We <u>are running out of</u> money.

（我們的錢快用完了。）

**y.** I <u>am looking forward to</u> hearing from you soon.

（我期待很快能得到你的回音。）

有時，三字片語動詞可由雙字動詞加上介系詞而形成，例如我們前面列出的 give up 可變成 give up on：

**z.** His parents <u>gave up on</u> him a long time ago.

（他的父母早就放棄對他的希望了。）

常見的三字片語動詞還有：

look down on「鄙視」

look up to「敬仰」

get along with「相處」

get away with「逃脫」

put up with「忍受」

catch up with「趕上」

get around to「處理」

boil down to「終歸」

go back on「食言」

close in on「包圍」

## 註解

1　片語動詞中的副詞常是所謂的介副詞。(有關介副詞的形成與用法，請參閱本系列文法書第三冊「形容詞與副詞篇」之第 1 章「副詞的種類」。)

2　事實上，片語動詞不僅限於兩個字，有些片語動詞包含了三個字（相關討論請見本章最後一節「三字片語動詞」），因此在本書中我們基本上不使用「雙字動詞」這個詞彙。

3　由於不及物片語動詞沒有受詞，因此並無可分離或不可分離的問題。

# 含介系詞的慣用語

　　英文的介系詞除了在文法上扮演「媒介」的功能之外，在日常口語中它們還是慣用語中不可或缺的要角。再上一章中我們已經看到它們在片語動詞中所擔當的「重責大任」，在本章中我們將看它們如何與其他詞類「合作」，形成母語人士經常使用的非動詞慣用語。

　　一般而言，較容易與介系詞產生關聯的除了動詞外，當然就是名詞了。的確，在包含介系詞的慣用語中絕大多數與名詞有關。但是，也有些慣用語中卻是介系詞與形容詞，甚至是副詞的組合。我們先討論由介系詞與名詞所組成的慣用語。

## 1 介系詞與名詞的組合

　　大部分由介系詞與名詞組合而成的慣用語呈現的是介系詞與受詞的關係，例如 at once、at times、by accident、for a change、in advance、in fact、on duty、on time、out of control、out of order、to the point、under arrest 等。請看例句：

**a.** You'd better come at once.

（你最好馬上過來。）

**b.** At times I feel like a fool.

（有時候我覺得自己像個傻瓜。）

**c.** We found him purely by accident.

（我們能找到他純屬偶然。）

**d.** Why don't we have some Japanese food <u>for a change</u>?

（咱們何不吃些日本料理換換口味？）

**e.** You need to pay us <u>in advance</u>.

（你必須先付錢給我們。）

**f.** <u>In fact</u>, I haven't seen her for years.

（事實上我已經好幾年沒看到她了。）

**g.** Who's <u>on duty</u> tonight?

（今天晚上誰值班？）

**h.** He is never <u>on time</u> for work.

（他從不準時來上班。）

**i.** The situation is getting <u>out of control</u>.

（情勢正逐漸失控。）

**j.** The elevator is <u>out of order</u>.

（電梯故障了。）

**k.** I don't understand what you're talking about – please get <u>to the point</u>.

（我不知道你在說些什麼——請講重點。）

**l.** "You're <u>under arrest</u>," the policeman said.

（那個警察說：「你被逮捕了。」）

介系詞與名詞也可以其他的組合方式出現，例如：

**m.** They fought <u>side by side</u>.

（他們並肩作戰。）

**n.** We go to see them <u>from time to time</u>.

（我們偶爾會去看他們。）

**o.** I'm trying to get <u>in touch with</u> him.

（我正試圖和他聯繫。）

另外，注意介系詞也可與代名詞組合成慣用語，例如：

**p.** <u>After all</u>, they were good friends.

（畢竟，他們是好朋友。）

**q.** She was sitting in the corner <u>by herself</u>.

（她孤零零地一個人坐在角落裡。）

其他常見的介系詞與名詞／代名詞組合而成的慣用語還有：

at first / last「最初／後」

at a loss「不知所措」

at present「目前」

(not) at all「全然（不）」

by all / no means「當然／絕不」

by the way「順便一提」

for good「永遠」

for the sake of「為了……的緣故」

from scratch「從零開始」

in common「共同的」

in particular「尤其」

in the long run「長遠來看」

in time「及時」

on behalf of「代表」

on hand「手頭上有」

on schedule「按預定時間」

out of date「過時的 / 地」

out of the question「不可能」

under age「未成年」

within limits「在有限範圍之內」

## 2 介系詞與形容詞的組合

相對於後接名詞的情況，在介系詞之後加形容詞或副詞顯得相當特別。我們先看幾個介系詞與形容詞的組合。

**r.** Those bank robbers are still <u>at large</u>.

（那幾個銀行搶匪仍然逍遙法外。）

**s.** He did not say <u>for sure</u> whether he would come or not.

（他並沒有明確地說要來或不來。）

**t.** <u>In general</u>, boys are taller than girls.

（一般來說，男孩子比女孩子高。）

**u.** I tried to persuade him, but <u>in vain</u>.

（我試圖說服他，但是徒勞無功。）

# 3 介系詞與副詞的組合

在介系詞之後使用副詞的情況較少。請看以下的例子：

**v.** We looked at them <u>from afar</u>.

（我們從遠處看他們。）

**w.** He pushed me <u>from behind</u>.

（他從後面推我。）

注意，也有在介系詞之前出現副詞的慣用語，例如：

**x.** <u>How about</u> some coffee?

（來點咖啡如何？）

**y.** <u>Away with</u> him!

（把他帶走！）

在本章中，我們嘗試從文法分析的角度來看英文的慣用語，但須知，既然是「慣用語」，它們本身就不須受嚴格文法的限制。這一點讀者可以稍加留意。

# 冠　詞

Articles

# 英文冠詞使用錯誤極可能立即產生溝通障礙。

## 1. 何謂冠詞？

什麼叫冠詞？冠者，帽也；簡單地說，冠詞就是「戴在名詞上的帽子」。英文把冠詞稱之為 "article"，由字根 arti (joint) 加上字尾 -cle (small；little) 所組成，指的也正是「必須連帶在名詞上的小字」，而這裡所謂的「小字」指的是相對於名詞這種「大字」（具明確語意內涵的「實詞」）的「功能詞」。那，為什麼英文的名詞要戴「小帽」呢？也就是說，英文的冠詞到底具備什麼功能呢？

須知，英文的名詞前常需要用限定詞 (determiner)，如 "this"、"that"、"my"、"your"、"some"、"any" 等，來表示該名詞的「指稱」(reference)。這一點對於以中文為母語的人而言，應該也會認為理所當然，因為中文都有相對應的字詞，且功能與意義皆相仿。但是，英文卻比中文多了兩個限定詞──定冠詞

(definite article) 與不定冠詞 (indefinite article)。有趣的地方在於，英文的名詞，如果沒有上列那些限定詞「明確地」表達出其指稱時，就需要「戴個帽子」。換個方式說，縱使說話者認為某個名詞的指稱無須特別明白表示時，他／她還是得在該名詞之前「貼個標籤」，至少標示一下這個名詞是「定」(definite) 還是「不定」(indefinite)。而這一點對於沒有冠詞的中文使用者而言，就容易造成困擾。試比較下面這兩個例子中的英文與中文：

① **The teacher** is coming!（老師來了！）
② He is **a teacher**.（他是老師。）

就英文的使用者而言，由於第一個例子裡的 teacher 是指特定的一位老師，因此必須在其前加上定冠詞 "the"；而在第二個例子裡的 teacher 只是用來說明主詞 He 的身分，並不具特定的意涵，所以加上不定冠詞 "a"。反過來講，對於使用中文的人來說，既然「老師」的指稱不須特別表明，那又何必畫蛇添足地加標示呢？*

## 2. 冠詞的重要性

一般學習英文的人可能會有一種錯覺，認為反正英文的冠詞只有兩個，隨便猜一下也有百分之五十「對」的機率。就考試而言，做錯做對幾道題目或許不致影響大局，但是在真正使用英文的時候，一個錯誤冠詞的使用卻極可能立即產生溝通上的

障礙 (communication breakdown)。比方說，你在一個陌生的地方，因為身體不適想找家藥房買些成藥吃，於是你就問某路人：Where is the drugstore?「（那家）藥房在哪裡？」對方肯定會覺得莫名其妙，而反問你一句：What drugstore?「什麼藥房？」你應該說的是：Is there a drugstore around here?「這附近有沒有藥房？」如此，對方便可以回答：Yes, there's one ....「有，……有一家。」或 No, there's no drugstore around here.「沒有，這附近沒有。」

又比如說，你我同在一個辦公室上班，我因為內急所以站起來跟你說：I'm going to a bathroom.「我要去上（某間）廁所。」你一定覺得很奇怪，認為我頭殼壞去，不知道我要跑到哪裡去上廁所，因為我們平常都是 "go to the bathroom together"「一起去上廁所」。

從以上兩個例子我們可以明顯感受到英文冠詞的使用在溝通時的重要性。切不可因為英文只有兩個冠詞而忽略了它們的存在。

在本書的第三部分中，我們將先說明「特定」與「不特定」這兩個概念，再依次討論定冠詞的用法、不定冠詞的用法，以及零冠詞與冠詞的省略。

---

[*] 或許這正反映出中、西在文化與思想上的差異：中國人較「善解人意」，既然「心照」也就「不宣」了；西方人重邏輯，實事求是，一是一，二是二，縱使麻煩也要把話說清楚、講明白。

Conjunction
Article
Preposition
and
which
who at
since
where over
a an
under
that

「特定」與「不特定」

　　一般文法書在討論冠詞時通常僅觸及表面，讀者學習到的大概就是諸如「如果一個名詞指的是特定的人事物時，其前就必須使用定冠詞；反之，則使用不定冠詞。」、「定冠詞用於特定名詞之前，不定冠詞則用於不特定名詞前。」等這類模糊籠統的「規則」了。對於什麼叫「特定」、什麼叫「不特定」的說明常常不夠清楚、明確，甚至付之闕如。因此，在我們討論定冠詞與不定冠詞的用法之前，有必要先釐清「特定」與「不特定」這兩個概念。

　　在前面「何謂冠詞」的說明中我們提到，英文的名詞前常用限定詞來表示「指稱」，[註1] 而所謂的指稱最基本的兩個概念就是「特定」與「不特定」。

## 1 特定的指稱

　　所謂特定的指稱 (definite reference) 指的是當說話者使用一個名詞時，該名詞的指稱對象 (referent) 非常明確，也就是，不論說話者或聽話者都知道該名詞指的是哪一個／些人事物。能夠用來表示特定指稱最典型的限定詞就是指示詞 (demonstrative)。請看例句：

**a.** This book is mine.
（這本書是我的。）

**b.** That one is yours.
（那本是你的。）

當然，指示詞也有複數形：

**c.** Who are these people?
（這些人是誰？）

**d.** Those guys are my friends.
（那幾個人是我的朋友。）

人稱代名詞的所有格形式 (possessive form) 也常用來表達特定的指稱。例如：

**e.** My son is in college now.
（我兒子現在在念大學了。）

**f.** Her daughter is still in elementary school.
（她的女兒還在念小學。）

**g.** I've never met your parents.
（我從來沒見過你／你們的父母。）

**h.** Their children have all grown up.
（他們的小孩都已經長大了。）

## 2 不特定的指稱

所謂不特定指稱 (indefinite reference) 指的是當說話者使用一個名詞時，該名詞並無明確之指稱對象的情況。常用來表示

不特定指稱的限定詞為數量詞 (quantifier)，例如 any、some、many，或數字詞 (cardinal number)，例如 one。請看例句：

**i.** Are there any letters for me?

（有沒有我的信？）

**j.** She bought some apples.

（她買了幾顆蘋果。）

**k.** Many women think they are overweight.

（很多女人認為自己過重。）

**l.** He lost one tooth in the fight.

（他在打鬥中掉了一顆牙齒。）

另外，有些疑問詞 (interrogative)，例如 what、which、whose，也可當作限定詞，用來表達不特定的指稱。請看例句：

**m.** What bus should we take?

（我們該搭什麼公車？）

**n.** Which one do you prefer?

（你比較喜歡哪一個？）

**o.** Whose car is this?

（這是誰的車子？）

在了解了「特定」與「不特定」這兩個概念之後，接下來我們就來看英文冠詞與兩者之間的關係。

## 3 由冠詞表達之「特定」與「不特定」

　　由冠詞所表達的「特定」或「不特定」與由其他限定詞所表達的「特定」和「不特定」基本上是相同的邏輯。不過，如前所述，由於中文沒有冠詞，因此國人在理解由英文冠詞所表達的指稱時，很容易產生困擾。最明顯的例子就是不知道該不該或該如何把定冠詞和不定冠詞「翻譯」出來。比如，"He is in the house." 是應該譯成「他在屋子裡。」還是「他在這／那間屋子裡。」？又比如，"My father is a doctor." 該譯成「我爸爸是醫生。」亦或「我爸爸是一個醫生。」？

　　其實，上面這兩個問題應該分兩個層次來看。首先，從理解以至於翻譯的角度，把 "the" 詮釋為「這個」(this) 或「那個」(that) 並非錯誤，因為中文沒有相對應的定冠詞，既然是一間「特定」的房屋，對中文的使用者而言，不是「這間」就是「那間」（端視說話者所在的位置）。至於把 "a" 當成「一個」也不能說不正確，因為 "a" 只能用在單數的可數名詞之前；換個方式說，在邏輯上 "a" 與 "one" 並不衝突。問題在於，我們可否就因此做以下的推論：

the ＝ this／that；a ＝ one

答案當然是否定的。雖然從語用 (pragmatics) 的角度來看，the、this、that、a、one 都是「限定詞」，但是在文法上，this、 that、one 屬於形容詞,具「修飾」名詞的功能;the 和 a 則爲冠詞,基本的功能僅在於「標示」一個名詞的指稱(即,特定或不特定)。

在確定冠詞與其他限定詞不同之後,接著我們就來看該如何正確使用冠詞。

## 4 冠詞的使用時機與條件

我們在前面提到過,如果說話者認爲一個名詞具特定的指稱但未用如 this、that、my、your 等限定詞來「限定」時,就必須使用定冠詞來標示;反之,若一個名詞的指稱不特定但無其他表達「非限定」之限定詞時,則需要用不定冠詞標示之。問題是,在不用或不適合使用明確的限定詞的情況下,說話者該如何做出判斷,使用正確的冠詞而不致產生溝通上的障礙呢?

首先,請比較一下下面兩個例子中的情境。

**p.** There is a dog outside. The dog looks big and fierce.

（外面有隻狗。那隻狗看起來又大又凶猛。）

**q.** Excuse me, where is the library?

（對不起,請問圖書館在哪裡?）

在 p. 例中說話者先告知對方在外面「有一隻狗」(There is a dog),然後再告訴對方該隻狗 (The dog) 如何如何;在 q. 例中說

話者直接問對方圖書館 (the library) 在哪裡。從語用的觀點來看，顯然 p. 例的說話者「知道」聽話者並不知道外面有一隻狗的存在，因此他先利用不定冠詞 "a" 製造了一個語境 (context)，而後在他使用定冠詞 "the" 之時，對方自然知道他指的就是前面提到的那隻狗；而 q. 例中的說話者既然直接了當地使用了定冠詞，一定是因爲他認爲聽話者知道他指的是哪一個圖書館（比如，兩人是同校的學生，而說話者是在跟聽話者問路）。換句話說，在 p. 例中說話者先用 "a" 來標示對方不知情況下的「不特定」指稱，再用 "the" 標示對方已知情狀況下的「特定」指稱；在 q. 例中，在說話者「認定」對方知情的情況下，他直接就使用了表「特定」指稱的 "the"。

我們再看一組對照的例子。

**r.** Let's find a boy to play this role. But the boy has to know how to sing and dance.

（咱們找一個男孩子來演這個角色。但是這個男孩一定得會唱歌、跳舞。）

**s.** Look, the bride is so beautiful.

（你瞧，新娘好漂亮。）

r. 例與上一組的 p. 例相同，說話者先建立一個他與聽話者間共通的語境——「找一個男孩」(find a boy)，然後再針對對方已經有了概念的「這個男孩」(the boy) 提出他認爲應有的條件。s. 例則與上面的 q. 例一樣，說話者在 bride 之前直接用 "the"，顯然他

認為對方知道他在講哪一個新娘（可能的情況是：說話者與聽話者參加同一場婚禮，在一起喝喜酒）。

但是，不知道讀者是否注意到了，事實上 r. 例與 p. 例並不完全相同。而這兩例的不同之處在於：p. 例的發話者說 "a dog" 時本身是知道自己指的是哪隻狗的（比如，他有可能是一面看著那隻狗一面講話），但是 r. 例的發話者本身並不知道他自己說的 "a boy" 究竟是哪一個男孩（因為還沒有去找）。在語用學上，p. 例中不定冠詞 "a" 的用法稱為「有所指」(specific)，[註2] 而 r. 例中不定冠詞 "a" 的用法則叫做「無所指」(non-specific)。[註3] 不過，不論說話者使用 "a" 時有所指或無所指，只要聽話者不知其所指就構成所謂的「不特定」指稱。

綜合以上的討論說明，我們可以清楚、簡單地歸納出英文冠詞的指稱與使用條件如下：

| 定冠詞 | 特定指稱 | ← 我知、你知 |
|---|---|---|
| 不定冠詞 | 不特定指稱 | ← A. 我知、你不知 (specific) |
| | | ← B. 我不知、你不知 (non-specific) |

（我＝說話者；你＝聽話者）

注意，冠詞的選擇取決於說話者；說話者必須判斷他即將使用的名詞指稱對方是否知曉。一旦判斷錯誤，結果不是產生誤解，就是造成溝通的中斷。

## 註解

**1** 限定詞的相關用法請參閱本系列文法書第二冊「名詞與代名詞篇」名詞部分之第 8 章「名詞片語」，以及第三冊「形容詞與副詞篇」形容詞部分之第 1 章「形容詞的種類」。

**2** 不定冠詞「有所指」的用法多出現在已知事實的陳述中，例如：

❶ He owned <u>a</u> company before.
（他以前擁有一家公司。）

❷ I have <u>a</u> son and a daughter.
（我有一個兒子、一個女兒。）

**3** 不定冠詞「無所指」的用法常出現在疑問、假設、否定等文句中，例如：

❶ Is there <u>an</u> ATM near here?
（這附近有沒有提款機？）

❷ If I were <u>a</u> king, I would ....
（假如我是個國王的話，我會……。）

❸ She doesn't have <u>a</u> boyfriend.
（她沒有男朋友。）

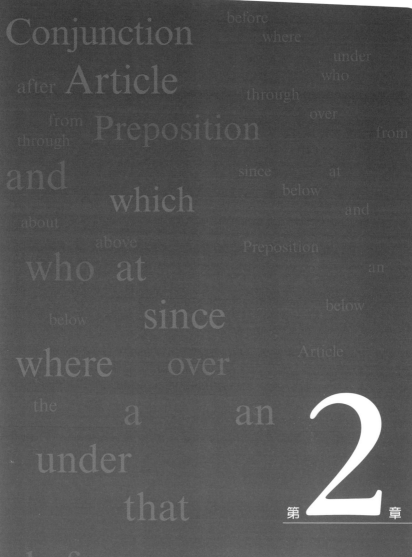

Conjunction
Article
Preposition
which
who at
since
where over
a an
under
that
before

第 **2** 章

# 定冠詞的用法

在上一章中我們從語用的角度討論了定冠詞與不定冠詞的使用原則，在本章中及下一章中我們將從傳統文法的角度分別審視定冠詞和不定冠詞的用法及應注意的事項。

以下我們分三部分來探討英文定冠詞的用法：「定冠詞的發音」、「定冠詞的一般用法」，及「定冠詞與專有名詞」。

# 1 the 的發音

定冠詞 the 有三種可能的發音：[ðə]、[ðɪ]、[ði]。

## A. 出現在以子音起頭的字前

當 the 出現在以子音起頭的字前時念成 [ðə]，例如：

the [ðə] man、the [ðə] dog、the [ðə] stupid man、the [ðə] big dog

## B. 出現在以母音起頭的字前

當 the 出現在以母音起頭的字前時念成 [ðɪ]，例如：

the [ðɪ] apple、the [ðɪ] orange、the [ðɪ] official name、the [ðɪ] average height

## C. 被強調而重讀時

當 the 被強調而重讀時念成 [ði]，例如：

the [ði] President、the [ði] only one

## 2 定冠詞的一般用法

除了我們在前一章提到的「語境」用法之外，下面幾個需要使用定冠詞的情況也必須特別注意。（許多考試都以它們為出題重點。）

## A. 在獨一無二的事物前必須用 the

例如：

the earth「地球」、the sun「太陽」、the moon「月亮」、the universe「宇宙」、the world「世界」、the sky「天空」

## B. 在方向或方位前必須用 the

例如：

the east「東邊」、the west「西邊」、the right「右邊」、the left「左邊」、the front「前面」、the back「後面」

## C. 在最高級形容詞前必須用 the

例如：

the greatest「最偉大的」、the happiest「最快樂的」、the most beautiful「最美麗的」

## D. 在序數前必須用 the

例如：

the first「第一」、the second「第二」、the third「第三」

## E. 在焦點形容詞前必須用 the

例如：

the only「唯一的」、the very「正是（那一個）」、the same「相同的」

## F. 在表達時間點或時間區隔的名詞前必須用 the

例如：

the beginning「開始」、the end「結尾」、the past「過去」、the present「現在」、the future「未來」

## G. 在表達以十年為期的年代時，必須用 the

例如：

the sixties「六〇年代」、the early seventies「七〇年代初

期」、the late nineties「九○年代末期」、the 1930's「一九三○年代」、the 2010's「二○一○年代」

## H. 在特定名詞前用 the 表群體、團體

例如：

the public「大眾」、the middle class「中產階級」、the police「警方」、the military「軍方」、the media「媒體」、the press「新聞界」

## I. 在表國民的名詞前用 the 表全體

例如：

the Chinese「中國人」、the Japanese「日本人」、the French「法國人」、the English「英國人」、the Americans「美國人」、the Italians「義大利人」、the Germans「德國人」[註1]

## J. 在單數普通名詞前用 the 可表該類之全體

例如：

the dog「狗」、the horse「馬」、the lion「獅子」、the tiger「老虎」[註2]

## K. 在單數普通名詞前用 the 可表該事物之抽象意義

例如：

the pen「文」、the sword「武」、the head「理性」、
the heart「溫情」

## L. 在某些形容詞前加 the 可指某一群人

例如：

the rich「富人」、the poor「窮人」、the young「年輕人」、
the old「老年人」、the dead「死人」

## M. 在某些形容詞前加 the 可指某一類事物

例如：

the impossible「不可能的事」、the unthinkable「不可想像
的事」、the supernatural「超自然現象」

## N. 在某些形容詞前加 the 可表抽象概念

例如：

the true「真」、the good「善」、the beautiful「美」

## O. 在某些分詞前用 the 可作複數名詞用

例如：

the living「活著的人」、the dying「垂死的人」、
the starving「挨餓的人」、the wounded「受傷的人」、

the disabled「殘障人士」、the disadvantaged「弱勢族群」

## P. 在某些分詞前用 the 可作單數名詞用

例如：

the unknown「未知之事物」、the unexpected「未預料之事物」、the untold「未說出之事物」、the unsolved「未解決之事物」

## Q. 在某些分詞前用 the 可作單數或複數名詞用

例如：

the accused「被告」、the deceased「死者」、
the insured「受保人」

## R. 在某些名詞前加 the 以作為計量單位

例如：

by the hour「以小時計算」、by the month「以月計算」、
by the pound「以磅計算」、by the gallon「以加侖計算」、
by the yard「以碼計算」、by the dozen「以打計算」

## S. 指彈奏樂器時，樂器名稱前須用 the [註3]

例如：

play the piano「彈鋼琴」、play the violin「拉小提琴」、
play the trumpet「吹喇叭」

## T. 指廣播（節目）時，radio 前須加 the

例如：

listen to the radio「聽廣播」、listen to the news on the radio
「收聽廣播新聞」註4

## U. 指身體部位時，常須用 the

例如：

injured in the leg「腿受傷」、hit in the head「打到頭」、
a pain in the chest「胸口疼痛」

## V. 在雙重比較結構中之比較級形容詞或副詞前須用 the

例如：

The more, the merrier.「多多益善。」
The sooner, the better.「愈快愈好。」

## W. 在以下與時間有關的慣用語中必須用 the

例如：

in the morning「早上」、in the afternoon「下午」、
in the evening「晚上」、in the daytime「日間」、in the
meantime「在此同時」、at the present time「目前」、
at the moment「此刻」、for the time being「暫時」、all the
time「始終」、all the while「一直」、in the long run「終究」

# 3 定冠詞與專有名詞

一般而言，專有名詞前不需要用冠詞，但是必須注意以下這些常與定冠詞 the 連用的專有名詞。

## A. 海、海洋之名稱

例如：

the Black Sea「黑海」、the Dead Sea「死海」、the Mediterranean Sea「地中海」、the Pacific Ocean「太平洋」、the Atlantic Ocean「大西洋」

## B. 海灣、海峽之名稱

例如：

the Gulf of Mexico「墨西哥灣」、the Persian Gulf「波斯灣」、the English Channel「英吉利海峽」、the Taiwan Strait「台灣海峽」、the Strait of Gibraltar「直布羅陀海峽」

## C. 河流名稱

例如：

the Yellow River「黃河」、the Mississippi River「密西西比河」、the Nile「尼羅河」、the Amazon「亞馬遜河」

## D. 山脈名稱[註5]

例如：

the Rocky Mountains（the Rockies）「落磯山脈」、the Himalaya Mountains（the Himalayas）「喜馬拉雅山脈」、the Alps「阿爾卑斯山脈」、the Andes「安地斯山脈」

## E. 群湖之名稱[註6]

例如：

the Great Lakes「五大湖」、the Finger Lakes「芬格湖」、the Virginia Lakes「維吉尼亞湖」、the Blue Lakes「藍湖」

## F. 群島之名稱[註7]

例如：

the Philippines「菲律賓群島」、the Pescadores「澎湖群島」、the West Indies「西印度群島」、the Bahamas「巴哈馬群島」、the Fiji Islands「斐濟群島」

## G. 半島名稱

例如：

the Balkan Peninsula「巴爾幹半島」、the Iberian Peninsula「伊比利半島」、the Korean Peninsula「朝鮮半島」、the Shandong Peninsula「山東半島」

## H. 沙漠名稱

例如：

the Sahara (Desert)「撒哈拉沙漠」、the Gobi Desert「戈壁沙漠」、the Taklamakan「塔克拉瑪干沙漠」、the Mojave「莫哈維沙漠」

## I. 地理位置名稱

例如：

the North Pole「北極」、the Equator「赤道」、the Northern Hemisphere「北半球」、the Middle East「中東」

## J. 國家名稱

例如：

the United States (of America)「美國」、the Republic of China「中華民國」、the Netherlands「荷蘭」、the Sudan「蘇丹」

## K. 城市名稱

例如：

the Hague「海牙」、La Paz「拉巴斯（波利維亞首都）」、El Paso「艾爾帕索（美國德州之城市）」[註8]

## L. 國際組織名稱

例如：

the United Nations「聯合國」、the European Union「歐盟」、the Red Cross「紅十字會」、the Rotary Club「扶輪社」

## M. 機關、單位等之名稱

例如：

the Legislative Yuan「立法院」、the Ministry of Education「教育部」、the State Department「國務院」、the Federal Burean of Investigation「聯邦調查局」、the Central Intelligence Agency「中央情報局」

## N. 建築物、橋樑等之名稱[註9]

例如：

the Empire State Building「帝國大廈」、the Statue of Liberty「自由女神像」、the Golden Gate Bridge「金門大橋」、the Brooklyn Bridge「布魯克林大橋」、the Eiffel Towel「艾菲爾鐵塔」

## O. 博物館、圖書館等之名稱

例如：

the Metropolitan Museum「大都會博物館」、the Louvre (Museum)「羅浮宮」、the National Palace Museum「故宮

博物院」、the Library of Congress「（美國）國會圖書館」、the National Central Library「（台灣）國家圖書館」

## P. 大學名[註10]

例如：

the University of Michigan「密西根大學」、the University of Pennsylvania「賓州大學（賓夕法尼亞大學）」、the University of London「倫敦大學」、the University of Tokyo「東京大學」、the University of Notre Dame「聖母大學」

## Q. 旅館名[註11]

例如：

the Ritz-Carlton Hotel「麗池卡爾登飯店」、the Spring Hotel「春天酒店」、the Ambassador Hotel「國賓大飯店」、the Grand Hotel Taipei「圓山大飯店」

## R. 船名、火車名

例如：

the Mayflower「五月花號」、the Titanic「鐵達尼號」、the Queen Elizabeth「伊莉莎白皇后號」、the Oriental Express「東方特快車」、the Taroko Express「太魯閣號」

## S. 時代、朝代等之名稱

例如：

the Stone Age「石器時代」、the Middle Ages「中世紀」、the Victorian Era「維多利亞時代」、the Han Dynasty「漢朝」、the Sung Dynasty「宋朝」

## T. 戰爭、運動等之名稱

例如：

the Civil War「南北戰爭」、the Sino-Japanese War「中日（甲午）戰爭」、the French Revolution「法國大革命」、the Women's Liberation Movement「婦女解放運動」、the Renaissance「文藝復興」

## U. 經典名

例如：

*the Bible*《聖經》、*the Koran*《可蘭經》、*the Book of Odes*《詩經》、*the Doctrine of the Means*《中庸》

## V. 報紙名[註12]

例如：

*the New York Times*《紐約時報》、*the Washington Post*《華盛頓郵報》、*the Baltimore Sun*《巴爾的摩太陽報》、*the China Post*《中國郵報》、*the China Times*《中國時報》

## 註解

**1** 注意，Americans、Italians 及 Germans 為複數形。

**2** 注意，man「男人」與 woman「女人」為例外，即使用來代表全體亦不加冠詞：

<u>Man</u> differs from <u>woman</u> in many ways.
（男人和女人在許多方面都不相同。）

**3** 注意，球類運動之前不用定冠詞，例如：play baseball「打棒球」、play tennis「打網球」、play football「踢足球」。

**4** 在 watch TV「看電視」、on TV「電視上」等片語中，不用定冠詞。

**5** 獨座的山則不須用 "the"，例如：Mount Everest「埃弗勒斯峰」、Mount Ali「阿里山」、Mount Fuji「富士山」。

**6** 單獨的湖不須用 "the"，例如：Lake Michigan「密西根湖」、Lake Superior「蘇必略湖」、Taihu Lake「太湖」、Sun Moon Lake「日月潭」。

**7** 單獨的島不須用 "the"，例如：Taiwan Island「台灣島」、Long Island「長島」、Bali Island「峇里島」、Puji Island「普吉島」。

**8** La Paz 中的 La 與 El Paso 中的 El 分別為西班牙文中的陰性及陽性冠詞，在英文中沿用原文。

**9** 有些建築物則不用定冠詞，例如：Carnegie Hall「卡內基（音樂）廳」、Rockefeller Center「洛克斐勒中心」、Sears Tower「希爾斯大廈」、Taipei 101「台北 101」。

**10**　有些大學名字不用 "the"，例如：Harvard University「哈佛大學」、Stanford University「史丹佛大學」、New York University「紐約大學」、Fu Jen Catholic University「輔仁大學」、National Taiwan University「台灣大學」。

**11**　有些旅館名字不用 "the"，例如：Shangri-La Hotel「香格里拉飯店」、Sheraton Hotel「喜來登飯店」、Hotel Royal「老爺酒店」、Grand Hyatt Taipei「台北君悅大飯店」。

**12**　注意，新聞性雜誌名多不用 "the"，例如：*Time*《時代雜誌》、*Newsweek*《新聞週刊》、*U.S. News & World Report*《美國新聞與世界報導》、*China Times Weekly*《時報週刊》。

Conjunction
Article
Preposition
which
who at
since
where over
a an
under
that
before

第 **3** 章

# 不定冠詞的用法

在本章中我們將分四個部分討論英文的不定冠詞：不定冠詞的拼法與發音、不定冠詞的一般用法、不定冠詞的特殊用法，以及包含不定冠詞的慣用語。

## 1 不定冠詞的拼法

在以子音開頭的字前，不定冠詞拼成 "a"，例如：

a book、a cat、a table、a great man、a strange woman

在以母音開頭的字前，不定冠詞拼成 "an"，例如：

an apple、an orange、an egg、an important day、
an ugly chair

注意，有些字在拼寫時以母音字母起頭，但是念以來卻是以子音開始，此時應用 a 而不用 an，例如：

a unit、a university、a European、a one-way street、
a useful tool、a unique（「獨一無二的」）building、
a unianimous（「全體一致的」）decision

相反地，有些字在拼寫時是以子音起頭，但是在念的時候卻是以母音開始，此時應用 an 而不用 a，例如：

> an hour、an honor、an M.A. [ˌɛm`e]、an X-ray [`ɛksˌre]、
> an honest person、an honorary（「榮譽的」）degree、
> an MP3 player

## 2 不定冠詞的發音

### A. a 的發音

一般弱讀時 a 念成 [ə]：

> a [ə] pen、a [ə] car、a [ə] teacher

當 a 被強調而重讀時念成 [e]：

> a [e] civilian、a [e] wonderful picture

### B. an 的發音

一般弱讀時 an 念成 [ən]：

> an [ən] idea、an [ən] engine、an [ən] author

要強調時 an 則念成 [æn]：

an [æn] accident、an [æn] unbelievable story

## 3 不定冠詞的一般用法

### A. 在無特定指稱之單數可數名詞前必須用 a 或 an

這種用法的 a 或 an 通常只用來表示某一人事物的屬性，而無其他特殊意義。請看例句：

**a.** John is a scientist.

（約翰是個科學家。）

**b.** A meeting is going to be held on Monday.

（星期一有一場會議要召開。）

**c.** Amy ate an apple.

（艾咪吃了一顆蘋果。）

### B. 以 a 或 an 來代替數字「1」

不定冠詞 a 或 an 可以用來表示「一」，例如：

**d.** He paid a hundred NT for the parking.

（他付了一百元新台幣的停車費。）

**e.** We waited an hour.

（我們等了一個鐘頭。）

## C. 以 **a** 或 **an** 表示同類的全體

不定冠詞 a 或 an 可用來表示同一類的人事物。請看例句：

**f.** A soldier must obey orders.<sup>註 1</sup>

（軍人必須服從命令。）

**g.** An eagle has very sharp eyes.<sup>註 2</sup>

（老鷹的眼睛非常銳利。）

## 4 不定冠詞的特殊用法

## A. 不定冠詞與不可數名詞

有時不可數名詞可轉作普通名詞用，若其意思指「一個」、「一種」等，則其前可用不定冠詞。<sup>註 3</sup> 例如：

**h.** Can I have a coffee, please?【物質名詞】

（麻煩你，我可不可以來杯咖啡？）

**i.** She showed an expected friendliness that surprised me.

【抽象名詞】

（她展現出一種令我驚訝的友善態度。）

**j.** He bought a Ford last week.【專有名詞】

（他上禮拜買了一台福特。）

另外，有時專有名詞加上不定冠詞可指「某一（位）」：

**k.** A Mr. Liu called you this morning.

（今天早上有個姓劉的先生打電話找你。）

## B. 不定冠詞 a 可與 most 連用，表示 very「很」

例如：

**l.** We spent a most enjoyable weekend in Yilang.

（我們在宜蘭度過了一個很愉快的週末。）

## C. 不定冠詞用來指 the same

例如：

**m.** Birds of a feather flock together.

（相同羽毛的鳥聚集在一起。／物以類聚。）

## 5 含不定冠詞的慣用語

英文的慣用語中常包含不定冠詞，而這些慣用語可分成「動

詞＋a＋名詞」與「介系詞＋a＋名詞」兩類。

## A. 動詞 + a + 名詞

例如：

make a living「謀生」、make a difference「使不同」、

take a break「休息」、take a picture「照相」、

do a favor「幫個忙」、give a hand「協助」、

catch a cold「感冒」、have a headache「頭痛」、

pay a visit「拜訪」、play a trick on「捉弄（人）」

## B. 介系詞 + a + 名詞

例如：

in a hurry「匆忙地」、in an instant「一瞬間」、

all of a sudden「突然地」、as a rule「照例地」、

as a result「結果」、as a whole「整體而言」、

at a loss「茫然」、on a diet「節食」、

for a while「一會兒」、with a view to「為了（做）」

## 註解

**1**　這個句子相當於下面兩句：

❶ Any soldier must obey orders.

❷ All soldiers must obey orders.

**2** 這個句子等同於下面兩句：

❶ The eagle has very sharp eyes.
❷ Eagles have very sharp eyes.

**3** 不可數名詞轉作普通名詞用的相關說明請參閱本系列文法書第二冊 「名詞與代名詞篇」之第一部分第 3 章「不可數名詞」。

Conjunction

before

where

Article

under

who

after

through

from

over

Preposition

through

from

and

since

at

below

which

and

about

above

who    at

Preposition

an

since

below

where    over

Article

the

a    an

under

that

4
第　章

before 零冠詞與冠詞的省略

在本書中我們把不需要冠詞的情況分成兩種：零冠詞 (zero article) 和冠詞的省略 (omission of articles)。[註1] 我們先討論零冠詞的情況。

## 1 零冠詞

所謂「零冠詞」指的是名詞本身原來就不需要冠詞的狀況。不須使用冠詞的名詞有下列八種。

### A. 複數的可數名詞[註2]

請看例句：

**a1.** Dogs and cats have been domesticated for a long time.
（狗和貓已經被馴養了很長的一段時間。）

**a2.** There are tables and chairs in the room.
（房間裡有桌子和椅子。）

**a3.** Boys are usually more active than girls.
（男孩子通常比女孩子好動。）

### B. 不可數的名詞[註3]

請看例句：

**b1.** This bridge is made of iron. 【物質名詞】

(這座橋是鐵做的。)

**b2.** He did that out of Kindness. 【抽象名詞】

(他那樣做是出於善心。)

**b3.** My name is Daniel. 【專有名詞】

(我叫丹尼爾。)

## C. 學科、語言名稱

請看例句：

**c1.** She majors in biology and minors in chemistry.

(她主修生物，副修化學。)

**c2.** I'm interested in philosophy and psychology.

(我對哲學和心理學有興趣。)

**c3.** He can speaks English, Spanish and Chinese.

(他會說英語、西班牙語和中文。)

## D. 運動名稱

請看例句：

**d1.** I play tennis twice a week.

(我一星期打兩次網球。)

**d2.** Football and baseball are outdoor sports.

(足球和棒球是戶外運動。)

## E. 餐名 註 4

請看例句：

**e1.** She sometimes skip breakfast.

（她有時不吃早餐。）

**e2.** I always go home for dinner.

（我都會回家吃晚飯。）

## F. 疾病名稱 註 5

請看例句：

**f1.** He contracted pneumonia and died.

（他得了肺炎死了。）

**f2.** Many people in Taiwan have hepatitis.

（台灣有很多人有肝炎。）

## G. 顏色名

請看例句：

**g1.** My favorite color is blue.

（我最喜歡的顏色是藍色。）

**g2.** She is dressed in red.

（她身穿紅衣。）

## H. 月、週日、假日名

請看例句：

**h1.** I was born in <u>August</u>.

（我是八月生的。）

**h2.** The boss is coming back on <u>Friday</u>.

（老闆禮拜五會回來。）

**h3.** Are you going home for <u>Thanksgiving</u>?

（你要回家過感恩節嗎？）

## 2 冠詞的省略

在以下這些狀況下，縱使一個名詞原需冠詞亦應將其省略。

## A. 用來直接稱呼對方的名詞前不用冠詞[註6]

請看例句：

**i1.** <u>Waiter</u>, can you get us some water?

（服務生，可不可以幫我們拿些水？）

**i2.** Listen to me, young <u>man</u>.

（聽我說，年輕人。）

## B. 用來稱呼家人的名詞前不用冠詞

用來稱呼家人的名詞前不用冠詞，但通常第一個字母要大寫，請看例句：

**j1.** Father will be home soon.

（爸爸很快就會回來。）

**j2.** I told Mother that I would be late.

（我跟媽媽說我會晚一點。）

## C. 用來表頭銜、身分的名詞前不用冠詞

用來表頭銜、身分的名詞前不用冠詞，尤其是當補語時，請看例句：

**k1.** They appointed her chairman of the board.

（他們指派她擔任董事長。）

**k2.** He was elected president of our class.

（他被選為我們班的班長。）

## D. 用來表活動、行為而非指場地本身的名詞前不用冠詞

請看例句：

**l1.** I went to bed at 11:30 last night.

（我昨晚十一點半就寢。）

**I2.** They are in <u>class</u> right now.

（他們現在正在上課。）

**I3.** She goes to <u>church</u> every Sunday.

（她每星期天都去做禮拜。）

**I4.** His father is in <u>prison</u>.

（他的父親在坐牢。）

### E. 在表示交通工具或運送方式的名詞前不用冠詞

在表示交通工具或運送方式的名詞前不用冠詞（注意，此時介系詞通常為 by），請看例句：

**m1.** They traveled by <u>train</u>.

（他們搭火車旅行。）

**m2.** I usually go to work by <u>bus</u>.

（我通常都搭公車上班。）

**m3.** We will ship the goods by <u>air</u>.

（我們會用空運運送這批貨。）

**m4.** Please send it by <u>registered mail</u>.

（請用掛號郵寄。）

### F. 置於 a / the / what kind of、a / the / what sort of、a / the / what type of 等之後的名詞不用冠詞

請看例句：

**n1.** What kind of <u>drink</u> would you like?

（你想喝哪一種飲料？）

**n2.** He is the sort of <u>guy</u> that you wouldn't like to work with.

（他是那種你不會想和他一起工作的傢伙。）

**n3.** She's a different type of <u>girl</u>.

（她是個不同型的女孩。）

## G. 兩個或兩個以上的名詞並列用來指同一人或物時，只在第一個名詞前使用冠詞，其他名詞前則不用冠詞

請看例句：

**o1.** The actor, <u>magician</u> and <u>novelist</u> is coming to Taiwan.

（那位演員兼魔術師與小說家即將到台灣來。）

**o2.** A watch and <u>chain</u> is usually expensive.

（鏈錶通常很貴。）

注意，由於以上二例中之主詞指單一人或物，故動詞用單數。<sup>註7</sup>

## H. 在採倒裝形式的讓步子句中，前移的補語不用冠詞

請看例句：

**p1.** <u>Child</u> as he was, he showed extraordinary courage.

（雖然只是個小孩，他卻展現出無比的勇氣。）

**p2.** <u>Woman</u> as she is, she's able to do whatever men soldiers can do.

（雖然她是個女人，任何男士兵能做到的她都能做到。）

# I. 用對等連接詞或介系詞聯結，呈對照關係的兩個名詞不需使用冠詞

例如：

husband and wife「夫妻」、father and son「父子」、
mother and child「母子」、question and answer「問答」、
bow and arrow「弓與箭」、heart and soul「心靈」、
day and night「日夜」、day after day「日復一日」、
face to face「面對面」、man to man「男人對男人」、
shoulder to shoulder「肩並肩」、hand in hand「手牽手」、
word for word「逐字」、step by step「逐步」、from headto
foot「全身上下」、from hand to mouth「僅能餬口」、
from beginning to end「自始至終」

# J. 在下列慣用語中的名詞前不需用冠詞

例如：

at noon「中午時」、at night「晚上」、at dawn「黎明時」、
at sunset「日落時」、at home「在家」、at work「在工作」、
on foot「步行」、on fire「著火」、in bed「在睡覺」、
in fact「事實上」、make sense「有意義」、

talk shop「談論本行」、take place「發生」、take part in「參加」、go to school「去上學」、come to class「來上課」、loose sight of「不再看得見」、give birth to「生（孩子）」

## 註解

**1** 多數文法書並不做如此區分。

**2** 當然，特定的名詞除外。

**3** 除非轉為普通名詞用，如前一章第四節中所提及之狀況。

**4** 當普通名詞用時除外。

**5** 但是在下列情況下需要冠詞：

❶ He has a cold / fever / headache.
（他感冒 / 發燒 / 頭痛。）

❷ She has the flu / mealsles / mumps.
（她得了流行性感冒 / 麻疹 / 腮線炎。）

**6** 在語言學上這樣用法的名詞稱為「呼格」(vocative)。

**7** 若每個名詞前皆有冠詞，則為複數主詞，意即

❶ The actor, the magician and the novelist are ....

❷ A watch and a chain are ....

# Notes

國家圖書館出版品預行編目資料

王復國理解式文法. 連接詞、介系詞與冠詞篇 / 王復國著.
　-- 初版. -- 臺北市：貝塔, 2011. 03
　　面：　公分

ISBN: 978-957-729-830-0（平裝）

1. 英語　2. 語法

805.16　　　　　　　　　　　　　　　　100003066

# 王復國理解式文法—連接詞、介系詞與冠詞篇
## Understanding English Grammar - Conjunctions, Prepositions & Articles

作　　者 / 王復國
執行編輯 / 朱曉瑩

出　　版 / 貝塔出版有限公司
地　　址 / 台北市 100 館前路 12 號 11 樓
電　　話 / (02)2314-2525
傳　　真 / (02)2312-3535
郵　　撥 / 19493777 貝塔出版有限公司
客服專線 / (02)2314-3535
客服信箱 / btservice@betamedia.com.tw

總 經 銷 / 時報文化出版企業股份有限公司
地　　址 / 桃園市龜山區萬壽路351號
電　　話 / (02)-2306-6842

出版日期 / 2017 年 10 月初版三刷
定　　價 / 250 元
I S B N / 978-957-729-830-0

貝塔網址：www.betamedia.com.tw

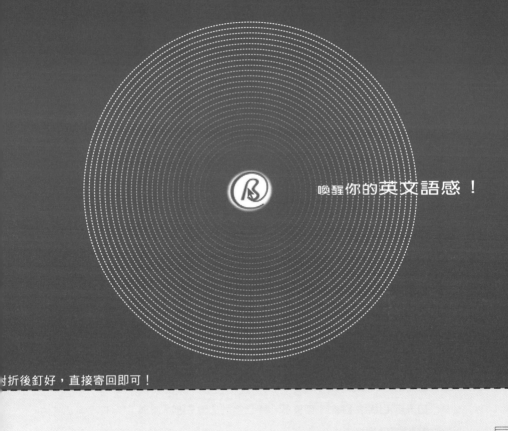

喚醒你的**英文語感**！

對折後釘好，直接寄回即可！

**100 台北市中正區館前路12號11樓**

貝塔語言出版 收
Beta Multimedia Publishing

寄件者住址 □□□

**貝塔語言出版**
Beta Multimedia Publishing

讀者服務專線（02）2314-3535　　讀者服務傳真（02）2312-353
客戶服務信箱　btservice@betamedia.com.tw

**www.betamedia.com.tw**

謝謝您購買本書！！

貝塔語言擁有最優良之英文學習書籍，為提供您最佳的英語學習資訊，您可填妥此表後寄回（免貼郵票）將可不定期收到本公司最新發行書訊及活動訊息！

姓名：_____　性別：□男 □女　生日：____年____月____日

電話：(公)_____(宅)_____(手機)_____

電子信箱：_____

學歷：□高中職含以下　□專科　□大學　□研究所含以上

職業：□金融　□服務　□傳播　□製造　□資訊　□軍公教　□出版

　　　□自由　□教育　□學生　□其他

職級：□企業負責人　□高階主管　□中階主管　□職員　□專業人士

1.您購買的書籍是？_____

2.您從何處得知本產品？(可複選)

　　　□書店 □網路 □書展 □校園活動 □廣告信函 □他人推薦 □新聞報導 □其他

3.您覺得本產品價格：

　　　□偏高 □合理 □偏低

4.請問目前您每週花了多少時間學英語？

　　　□ 不到十分鐘 □ 十分鐘以上，但不到半小時 □ 半小時以上，但不到一小時

　　　□ 一小時以上，但不到兩小時 □ 兩個小時以上 □ 不一定

5.通常在選擇語言學習書時，哪些因素是您會考慮的？

　　　□ 封面 □ 內容、實用性 □ 品牌 □ 媒體、朋友推薦 □ 價格□ 其他_____

6.市面上您最需要的語言書種類為？

　　　□ 聽力 □ 閱讀 □ 文法 □ 口說 □ 寫作 □ 其他_____

7.通常您會透過何種方式選購語言學習書籍？

　　　□ 書店門市 □ 網路書店 □ 郵購 □ 直接找出版社 □ 學校或公司團購

　　　□ 其他_____

8.給我們的建議：_____

_____

喚醒你的英文語感！

Get a Feel for English !

喚醒你的英文語感！

Get a Feel for English !